P9-DMO-655

VIETNAM

BOOK THREE

FREE-FIRE ZONE

CHRIS LYNCH

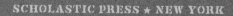

SCHOLASTIC PRESS ★ NEW YORK

ISBN 978-0-545-49427-4

10 9 8 7 6 5 4 3   14 15 16
        Printed in the U.S.A.   23
    This edition first printing, September 2012

        The text type was set in Sabon MT.
        Book design by Christopher Stengel

CHAPTER ONE

Ready Rudi

Everything counts.

That's the difference, here. That's the difference between life now and here and life before and everywhere else. Nothing really counted before.

There were two kinds of results back there back then, meaning my previous, pre-Marines life. There were two kinds of results, and those were *failure* and *that didn't count*. Usually, failure. But if I actually passed a quiz, the quiz was too easy so that didn't count. If I got a base hit, the sun was in somebody's eyes so that didn't count. If I pitched a penny closer to the wall than anybody else, then I must have stepped over the line or the wall moved or whatever so that didn't count and so just do it over again, *Rudy-Judy*. Course, nobody called me Rudy-Judy if my buddy Ivan was around, except sometimes Ivan, but the rest was always the same:

We weren't ready, Rudi, so it don't count. Do it over. You gotta do it over.

Now? I never need to do it over. And you have to be ready. 'Cause it counts, brother. It all counts now.

"Can you *count*, private?!"

"Yes, *forty-three*, sir, I, *forty-four*, can."

I can't believe how happy I am in this situation. There's a big beast of a baldy-man drill instructor spitting in my face while I do push-ups in the strongest sun I've ever dealt with. There could even be two suns working on me from two angles, because that's how the summer sun feels here in the South. The DI, who is a sergeant, is doing the push-ups with me, which is kind of decent of him in the suns and everything, and the spitting is not at all intentional. At least I don't think so.

See, I was doing my push-ups like he told me to and something got him riled, like lots of things do, and he hit the dirt with me, stretching out in the opposite direction. His feet are down that way and mine are back behind me like they usually are, and our faces are together, going up and down at the same time while he screams and spits at me, which he calls *chatting*. We've had a lot of chats, me and him. Guys are standing lined up beside me in both directions and laughing, which usually isn't allowed, but Sarge made a special Rudi Rule after the first two weeks of camp that it was okay to laugh at me. Because recruits could not afford to be expending the considerable energy it would take to *not* laugh at me while that energy was going to be needed elsewhere.

I'm kind of a legend here in the South.

And by "here in the South," I don't mean someplace like Marshfield or Woods Hole, either. I mean Parris Island, South Carolina, where guys say the Devil himself goes for his summer vacation.

"I don't believe that you *can* count, private!"

Sarge is in great shape, to be doing the push-ups in the suns and still screaming like he is.

"I can, *fifty-two*, sir. Just not, *fifty-four*, real great."

The guys are busting out laughing now and who even knows why. But it's fun. Sarge even goes way out of line and lets himself fall chest-flat on the ground while I keep pumping and the guys keep laughing.

"Are you for real, private?"

He's got me with that one. I keep on pushing up, trying to keep count in my head, trying to come up with an answer to his question, trying to keep the guys laughing at the same time because I like that and the sergeant surely likes that and when he's happy everybody's happy.

I've never felt so powerful in all my life, I swear. My head is swimming with it.

Until my arms buckle under me and my face bounces off the baked dirt of the ground.

Some time passes. That's not a big deal of course, since time does that kind of thing all the time. But the difference now is, this time passes without me. Because when I open my eyes, without remembering ever closing them to begin with, I am indoors, sitting in a chair. Everything's all changed from the last moment I remember — except for Sarge being right in my face.

"I do have to ask you again," he says, a lot less screamy and tough than usual, "are you for real, recruit?"

"No, sir," I say, "I'm only drafted."

Behind Sarge, somebody chuckles. That somebody turns out to be the medic, who brushes past Sarge and leans close to me. He's checking out my eyes, feeling my skull and my nose.

"Where you from, kid?" he asks. He has a strong accent, like he's a local around here, even though nobody seems to actually be from Parris Island, South Carolina. The only guys who say they're from Parris Island are the Marine recruits, and they're all actually from someplace else. Like me, for instance.

"I'm from Boston, sir."

Sarge cuts in. "And we thought it was all clever college boys up in Boston."

"It is," I say. "The smart ones are all still there."

They both laugh now, and Sarge reaches in to slap my leg. "Well, that's good. I'm glad they off-loaded you on us, then. You gonna be all right?"

I look to the medic, since it seems to me he's the one making that decision. But his answer is way too long. At some point he says something like "heat frustration," which sounds too much like something I would say, so I won't be saying it.

I definitely hear the last part, because he's looking at me when he says it. "If he learns to keep hydrated — and learns to count — he should be just fine," he says.

Turns out Sarge only asked me for thirty push-ups. I really must pay closer attention.

"Anyway," I say, "it's not like I'm ever gonna run into any hotter sun than South Carolina sun, that's for sure."

They both go quiet, staring at me, though I don't know what I've done wrong this time. Then they turn to each other.

"Is he for real?" the medic asks Sarge.

Sarge has a big smile on his face, though he's also shaking his head as he asks me:

"Recruit, have you ever heard of a place called *Vietnam*?"

CHAPTER TWO

Shooting Solves

Fire.

The place is on *fire*.

I apologize to both countries, but they shouldn't be called *North Vietnam* and *South Vietnam*. They should be called *North Fire* and *South Fire*.

Here's a joke. It was told to me by a guy on the troop ship that brought us here from Oakland, California. He was coming back this way after serving one tour of duty, getting discharged, going home, then signing up again when he got bored with life outside the war because it had very little shooting and stuff like that.

The joke is: What's the difference between an oven on full blast and summer in Vietnam?

And anyway, I forgot the answer, so the answer is: nothing. There is no difference, okay?

Fire. The feel of fire is everywhere, heat rising up off the ground and pouring down from the sky, and it seems like half of everything is *actually* on fire half the time, from the bombs and the napalm, and I swear the temperature goes *down* when you get close to real, flamey-type fire instead of standing in the regular open air of Vietnam.

Fire!

You hear the word all the time, too. They really encourage a lot of shooting. I find myself constantly comparing what I do here with what I might've been doing back in Boston, and I can never see anybody letting me shoot at anything over there. I have to say, right off the bat that makes it Marines 1, regular life 0.

'Cause it's hot in combat terms, too. Has been from the day I arrived in I Corps Tactical Zone — that's the north part of South Vietnam, just to be extra confusing. Getting to camp was like a tour of every kind of destruction you could imagine. And then I didn't even make it to lunchtime on day one before I was sent out with a patrol and orders to shoot at everything that moved.

Nothing moved. We shot anyway. At trees and hills and clouds and abandoned burned-out vehicles.

I have to say, I like the shooting.

I like the *war*.

I shouldn't say that. Even I know I shouldn't say that. Nobody should like a war, even if they are great at it, like General Patton or Snoopy or somebody. But this is so different from life the way it was. And those are the only two ways of life I have to compare.

I was all wrong back home, and that's the truth.

I'm all right here.

I haven't killed anybody yet — not for sure, but I've tried. And almost as good as a confirmed kill is when you fire your M-16 in the direction of the enemy and you actually see them run away, run like rabbits, this way and that because they are *afraid*. Just a week ago, some fighters from the other side ran away screaming in another language when my company took over this village full of Vietcong and their sympathizers and, man, there's nothing, like nothing, that compares with that anywhere in my experience. I was heavy breathing for about an hour after that excursion, and I wasn't even tired. Getting kind of breathy right now just remembering. If they'd shot back instead of retreating, I think my lungs might have broken my ribs.

I'm scared, too, so it's not like I'm saying I'm not. But that's a whole other thing. I'm scared, but a little bit less than yesterday and a little bit less than the day before and a good lot less than at the start of my eight weeks of basic training. So the direction I'm going seems to be the right one.

And I was scared a whole bunch of the time in Boston, too. Difference is that when something scares me here, I shoot at it. You know what those fleeing, screaming, scaredy VC looked like to me? A bunch of ol' Rudi-Judies, is what they looked like. Made me want to shoot 'em all the more.

I haven't killed any just yet — not confirmed. But it's only a matter of time.

Shooting solves a lot of stuff, it really does.

CHAPTER THREE
Cabbage

Lieutenant Jupp is our squad leader and for the most part he is not popular, though I like him okay.

"Boiled Cabbage, get over here, now!" he yells at me from across the camp. He speaks the opposite way most people do, in that he screams all his words unless he's very angry. Or unless he has a good reason not to, I guess, like if we're on patrol and screaming gets us noticed and located and dead. He started calling me Boiled Cabbage — or just Cabbage, or BC — practically as soon as he saw me. Never told me why, but I figure it's due to the fact I wear green and I have my helmet on almost every minute because I like the way it makes me feel. And also apparently my face is a kind of boiled red all the time since I arrived in-country.

My mom used to sing this song sometimes, when she was cooking. "Oh, I'm a savage / for bacon and cabbage . . ." Made me laugh. I miss her bacon and cabbage more than most of the rest of life at home.

"Yes, sir, lieutenant," I say, as I always say. I'm up off my bunk and out of the hooch as I say it. A hooch is a sort of structure with the frame of a house and the everything else of a tent. Lt. Jupp is across the yard in his own quarters, but I never miss a call. Like a dog to a whistle, the other guys say, but I say it's like a Marine to an order.

I like orders. Good Marines are great at following them.

"Can I give you a job, Cabbage?" he barks as I stand just inside his hooch and he hunches over a small writing table covered in maps.

"Yes, you can, sir," I say.

"Of course I can. But can I give you a job and be sure it gets done and gets done right and nobody gets accidentally killed or maimed including yourself?"

He's shouting all these words, so all the camp is listening and there are laughs here and there and a few comments, some guys shouting stupid answers pretending to be me.

"Yes, sir," I say.

"Good!" He barks that one real loud, because when he has only one syllable to get out he likes to get it *way* out. "Private, I would like you to lead the squad out to this spot here on the map. . . ."

Urrrr.

As much as I love following orders, my head gets a lot swimmy at this part. I can't stand reading maps. I mean, every little colored line on a map might just as well be one more thread of choke wire and all of them wrapping around my brain and pulling tight. And so I panic, privately to myself.

"Are you listening to me, private?" he bellows. So maybe possibly the panic's not completely private to myself.

"Yes, sir, I'm listening." I'm listening with all my might.

We're supposed to go and visit a village about eight miles down the road from Chu Lai, where we're stationed. We've been to the village before, even, a few times. The assignment is simple as simple can be, kind of like my mom sending me to the store for sugar and tea and margarine like she was doing by the time I was five. Lt. Jupp wants us to march down to what we call Co Co Village and hook up with the CAP unit we have living up there. CAP is for Combined Action Program, where whole units of Marines live full-time with real Vietnamese in their own villages. The idea is to keep the Vietcong out, and to kinda keep us in. Even though we're on their side, it's not always sure how much the

South Vietnamese love us being here, so it pays to stay on top of it.

"Candy!" Lt. Jupp says.

"Candy, sir," I say, because a Marine does not have to understand a thing to repeat it.

"We have come into possession of a shipment of candy. And some flower seeds. And vegetable seeds. And some Captain America comic books and assorted whatnot that we do not particularly need but that will undoubtedly help out the CAP effort down at Co Co. I want you men to deliver these goods, moving along this trail here mostly by the river. Get you some badly needed activity, as well as maintaining that road clean and safe for us between here and there."

Things have been very quiet in the area lately. Nothing too exciting going on, so we've done a lot more lying around and listening to the war in the far distance than we have soldiering. It won't last, of course, and we're supposed to remain battle-ready and fit, not lazy.

"You won't be coming with us then, sir?"

"No, Cabbage, I thought this is just the kind of beginner operation I would like to see you leading for yourself. Then someday, who knows, we might be able to take your training wheels off."

It's stupid how excited that statement makes me. I should be embarrassed, is what I should be, but I'm not. Of the twelve of us in the squad, I would be the dead twelfth in a map-reading competition. If you split the next stupidest guy in two, I would come in thirteenth. Heck, our squad is divided into two fire teams and we almost never even see those guys but I am sure every last one of them beats me at map reading. If I went to look for them to find out, I'd just get lost.

But everybody already knows the way to Co Co. Even I know the way. Once the map became part of the deal, my senses went inside-up and outside-down, but I'd be fine out on the road and mapless.

Candy delivery.

At least I'm smart enough to know I should be a little embarrassed. But I'm dumb enough to be proud and excited as well.

He likes me. More than he likes any of the other guys. He favors me and has done right by me from the start, like he wants to try and make some small something out of me while we're here.

I won't let him down.

The sounds when I walk back into the hooch could just as easily be coming all the way from seventh grade. I'm getting bombarded with *oooohhh*s and *hooooo*s and loud, smacking kissing noises. It's enough to make me freeze there in the door frame and flame red all over, just like grade school was six seconds ago and not six years.

"What?" I say to the guys, with my hands held out and my face probably screwed in four different expressions. I love to be part of the squad, love it, and if that means taking some grief, then I love grief. But my faces are surely also telling how confused and a little nervous I am, because some of this is fun and some of it is nasty and, like with everything around here, it's at least a little threatening.

Private Marquette hops up off his bunk and comes right up to me, getting in my face with all that fun and scary all at once as he says loud, "The *candy run*? Cabbage, man, you're leading us on the *candy run*?"

"I guess you heard," I say.

"King Candy — that should be your new nickname, Cabbage. You far too sweet to be any ol' cabbage. And don't the boss know it."

"Teacher's pet right there," Gillespie says, sitting on the side of his bunk with his shirt off and his new Marine Corps *Semper Fidelis* tattoo still glowing sore red on his left pectoral muscle.

Teacher's pet. Me.

"First time I've ever been called *that*, I can tell ya," I say, as truthful a thing as I'll say all day.

Since being stationed in Chu Lai, I'd have to say my experience of the war hasn't been quite what I pictured in terms of the personnel and command structure.

People sort of do what they feel like, much more of the time than I would have guessed.

"Do you think the corporals might have wanted to join us?" I ask as we start down the road — the mighty five of us who decided to march.

Right behind me, the guy we call Squid gives me a shove in the back with what feels like the nose of his gun. His head is squid shaped, but he's still one of the better guys.

"Since you've been here, Cabbage, have the corporals wanted to do anything?"

"Well," I say, "no. But delivering candy is a pretty decent job, and the weather's okay, and it's been really boring lately. . . . Hey, Squid, stop with the poking. You're gonna wind up shooting me."

"Sure, kid. Anyway, the corporals have a fun job today. They get to play with our prisoner."

We actually captured a guy a few days earlier. Though it's hard to even really call it *capture* since he more or less staggered into camp and found our hooch at random. He was delirious, unarmed, and just took an empty bunk for himself.

"What're they doing with him?" I ask.

"Questioning him," Gillespie says. "This is the first day he's been able to speak. He's gotta be a nobody, though, or the real interrogation boys would keep him for themselves."

I'd like to interrogate somebody, no matter how much of a nobody he is. Any job they let me do I'm gonna do, because I want to learn everything about this profession, do everything it's possible to do within it.

Right now, what there is to do is march. It's a well-worn southerly road we travel, with the two kinds of Vietnam War basically split fore and aft of us. Behind us, beyond Chu Lai, then past Da Nang and the city of Hue, lies North Vietnam and the North Vietnamese Army and the kind of straight-up war America's been fighting for a long time. There are tanks and planes and lots and lots of grunts in open firefights.

In front of us, and all the way down through the whole of South Vietnam, is the other thing. Or other *things*. It starts out simple enough: We're fighting alongside the South Vietnamese army, the ARVN, against the communists.

That's the only thing I can tell you for sure about the war in the South. And honestly, I can't even tell you that for sure.

Because it's nothing like any movie war I've ever seen, where one side fights the other side from their own side trying to take the other side. Here, if there was a traffic cop, say, directing war traffic, that cop would be like the Scarecrow in *The Wizard of Oz* when he was nailed up on that pole at the crossroads. *Well, if you want to fight the North Vietnamese Army, you'll want to go this way*, he would say, one arm pointing up in the general direction of Hanoi. *Or, if you want to fight the National Front for the Liberation of South Vietnam — the Vietcong — try this way*, and then about seventeen million arms would shoot out from his other side and point every single which way all over the place. They'd be pointing at the trees, the rice paddies, the villages, the little sampan boats, into tunnels, or into the city at the young local man sitting right next to a Marine sipping tea in a café.

For one thing, that kind of fighting is very different, scattered and secret and sly and scary.

For another thing, "Liberation of South Vietnam?" I thought that's what *we* were doing? Liberate them from who?

The march is without incident — but then, it seems like the most disastrous ones always start that way. All the horror stories I hear from guys who come and go — and they come and go from our base every day — are ones where it's creepy quiet and then some horror happens. The *bang-bang*-shoot-'em-up stories play out a lot simpler.

I have about fifty pounds of candy on my back, and that is a story I never figured I'd bring back from this place. By the time we make it all the way down the road, the march has eaten up over two hours and the guys behind me have eaten up probably eight pounds of candy from my pack. The trail, predictably and thankfully, was quiet. Nobody shot at us, we didn't shoot at anybody else, and as we sweep into Co Co Village, the candy is safe and sweet, and we are popular.

"Gentlemen," says the CAP unit leader, Sergeant Culverhouse. He's been expecting us, and as always we're a welcome sight. It's a kind of perfect relationship we have with these guys. Like Santa Claus we sweep in, drop off treats, then sweep out again without ever asking for anything in return.

The kids of the village have caught on to this as well, and they rush up and surround us as we begin to empty our packs of the goodies.

There are so many kids under the age of five in this village, I sometimes wonder if it's a tiny little society of their own. Of the half dozen or so times I've been here, I've seen up close maybe twenty-five adults, and three or four times that many little ones. Of the adults, none seem to be fighting-age males. Instead, the place is populated with women and old guys. There's a whole company of Marines stationed here, but really, if the locals decided to revolt, all but about three of our guys could just stay in bed for it.

Being popular, by the way, is nice.

When the kids figure out which bags have treats, the best kind of mayhem breaks loose. The sergeant backs away, like his post is being overrun and he's surrendering. Three little boys, barefoot and shirtless, lead a pack of maybe a dozen kids. They swamp Marquette, topple him, and tear open his bag while he laughs away on all fours. They make short work of him, realize he's carrying nothing but seeds and powdered plant food, and drop him like yesterday's news. One by one, our little detail of five gets the same rough treatment until the jig is finally up and the two of us carrying the mother lode, me and Private Hunter, get the full ransack.

I can't help laughing my head off as I get completely brutalized by these little guys and gals. I'm watching Hunter surrender to both the rough stuff and the laughter and it just makes me laugh more. The other guys stand around over us, like the old days in the school yard when a fight was on, and cheer the little ruffians into more and more of a frenzy.

"And wait 'til the little beasties get some of that sugar into them," Culverhouse says.

"It won't make them fat, that's for sure," Hunter says.

That's the truth. There's not one ounce of extra meat on any of these kids, but I swear I couldn't get up now if they didn't want me to. There's strength in these hard little bodies that I don't think I ever knew when I was that small. They're tough and determined, and despite the Christmas-ness of what's going on, there's not a whole lot of laughs on their side. This is a serious operation, I realize as the last of the kids clear out the last of the goodies, and serious is how they're taking it.

I find myself sitting upright on the ground as the invading army disperses with the spoils of war. Sgt. Culverhouse takes inventory of all the rest of the stuff — the comics, the seeds, and playing cards and yo-yos and soaps and all the assorted items of donation from whatever source sent it. Nothing in our delivery is too hugely necessary for sustaining life, but all of it's designed to improve it just a little bit.

"This'll go a long way," Culverhouse says as he assigns several villagers the task of moving it all wherever it needs to go. The sergeant speaks in what sounds to me like pretty confident Vietnamese — though it could just as well be a made-up language for all I know. I watch these folks, one older man and three women, interacting with the sergeant in a way that seems warm and polite and grateful and familiar but still, I don't know . . . foreign? *Foreign* is the word I would use. It's one of the more amazing bits of the war to me, the CAP program, and I can see here how and why it might work. It's practical. It seems like it has good intentions. And with the right people at the helm, people like Sgt. Culverhouse, I could see where it could do our most critical job — what they call "winning hearts and minds" — better than any other approach.

And then. And then, as I look at the interaction again, I think: I could never do this. I could never *understand* such foreign people the way we need to understand them.

I guess that's why I'm not a CAP guy.

Suddenly, the calm and nice gets smacked right off the board by angry shouting, in both English and Vietnamese and possibly in French, coming from a hut about thirty feet away. I get up and run a few steps behind the sergeant as he chases after it. I look back over my shoulder and notice none of my guys are as curious about this as I am.

They've all been in-country longer than me.

"What, what, what?" Culverhouse shouts as he steps into the hut.

"He knows something, sarge," the Marine inside snaps. In front of him, kneeling down, is an old Vietnamese man, who looks to me to be snarling up at the Marine. Though he also has his hands folded, like he's praying, or like he's pleading.

The sergeant stands there, taking it in, not appearing overly concerned. I take a step past him, farther into the small circular hut, where I have an equal view of everybody. The man on the ground says something — it sounds French — and the Marine growls furiously before punching the old guy right in the forehead, knocking him over backward.

"He knows what?" I blurt, shocked into butting in where I bet I'm not welcome.

The Marine turns to me, twists his face into a look of total shock at my ignorance. "Well, I don't know yet, do I? That's why I'm smacking him, stupid."

I turn to the sergeant again. He looks impassive. I turn back to the others in time to see the Marine pulling the man back up into kneeling position. He looks at the sergeant while he does it.

"Who's the melon, anyway, sarge?" Meaning, me.

"Delivery boy from Chu Lai," he says flatly.

So *that's* what I am.

The Marine smacks the man again, the man goes down again, and when he pulls him back up this time he presses the tip of a small local-type spear into that little cutout between the man's collarbones.

I've seen a few of these spears — Punji sticks — that guys have taken off of VC. Smelled them, too. The VC dip them in some kind of animal waste to give a guy the extra treat of infection along with the puncture.

"Krug," Sergeant says, "that's probably enough for now." Then, to me, "Old guy's VC."

"How do you know that?" I ask.

I realize there's a way you can ask a question like that — *How do you know that?* — that can sound punky, really get up a guy's nose. But that is not how I ask. It is a genuine attempt by one Marine to learn something from another.

Sarge clearly doesn't hear it that way.

"We are professionals," he says in a way that gives me the first chill I've had since I arrived in this part of the world. "And you are dismissed, private."

And just like that, dismissed I am.

CHAPTER FOUR

Hearts and Minds

Because of how slow things've been, I'd hoped to spend a little more time in Co Co. It would be good to learn about the local population, both from the people themselves and from the *professionals* who are putting so much into figuring them out. And, to be honest, I wouldn't have minded stretching out that moment of welcome and appreciation that we got from bringing goodies. For a minute it felt like those old news reels I used to watch of World War II Marines getting all the love from the world wherever they went. That hasn't happened here in this world and in this war as much as I'd hoped.

But the welcome mat is not out. It's a lesson I'm learning quick and hard, that moods change around here without the normal-world kind of warnings. You're a friend — you're a foe on account of a look — a word — a gesture that somehow questions something you shouldn't be questioning and that puts you on the other side of a line you didn't even know was drawn.

"Thank the lieutenant for me," Sgt. Culverhouse says in a thankless way. I'm walking past my guys, who look confused, then catch on, falling in behind me.

Nobody had really planned on starting another eight-mile hike so soon after the previous eight-mile hike, but after about two seconds nobody looks entirely shocked about it, either. Like I said, they've all been here longer than me.

"Hearts and minds," Squid says, as we start single-filing back northward.

"We win the hearts while we lose our minds," Marquette adds. It's the first time I've heard it, but it is obviously not the first time they've said it.

We're maybe getting a little soft, a little casual due to all the lack of activity we've been enduring. *Lacktivity* is the term the guys have been using. But it may very well be an enemy ploy, and if it is it's an effective one because about three miles into the drudge of our march back, we are one hundred percent surprised when we walk practically right into two of our guys.

"Boo," says Corporal Cherry, catching us so off guard he's already laughing loudly by the time we draw weapons. A normally functioning Marine squad would have shredded him with M-16 fire before he could've stopped us, but we're clearly far from our sharpest selves. And he knows that. He wasn't even worried.

"Jeez," Gillespie says, panting. "Cherry, man, you could have gotten yourself killed, and maybe us, too, acting the fool like that."

Cherry just shakes his head at our lameness. He's sitting in plain view, on a boulder the size of a Volkswagen.

"Boo," says Corporal McClean, from against a tree on the opposite side of the road.

"Jeez again," says Gillespie.

"Man," McClean says, "I knew it was bad, but this is beyond bad. You guys could be taken out by a troop of Girl Scouts throwing cookies."

He is so right.

This is humiliating, even if these two seem to think it's just a laugh.

The mood. The thing I noticed, about the quick shift of moods in this strange and unusual place, is happening to *me* now. I feel it, am completely aware of it as it comes over me. I'm embarrassed and furious and petrified and enraged over what just happened, didn't happen, might have happened.

The guys are all laughing. Big joke, right?

But it's no joke. No joke at all. We're trained fighting men. We were prepared for a purpose, by the most lethal fighting force the world has ever known, and when the moment came we were pathetic.

I am pathetic.

I march. There are two corporals here now and so there is no way I am actually in charge anymore, but so what. Who cares? If we can't keep our heads up, our wits about us, our weapons at the ready, then really, what are we and what matters at all?

"Cabbage," Cpl. McClean says, catching up to me. I hear the soft *pat-pat* of boots falling in line behind us.

I keep marching, just like I was taught. Crisp, strong, focused.

"What's the problem, Cabbage?"

"I should be dead," I say. "We should all be dead. You're right. Girl Scouts could take us."

"Aw," he says, slapping my back too hard, "don't be so tough on yourself. Lesson learned, right? Guys lose their edge pretty quick when the action falls off. And really, what's the point of staying on alert and all gung ho all the time, anyway? Look around, son. Nobody in all of I Corps is taking this seriously anymore. Just keep your head down and get your year in-country over with. If you kill some Vietnamese, that's a bonus, but what you're really here to kill is time."

There's so much that's wrong with this. What is he saying? Why is he saying it? Why is he saying it to *me*? There are a lot of quirky personalities in the Marines, in Chu Lai, in I Corps, and in all of Vietnam, but none of them are quirkier than our corporals. This is the longest conversation I've had with either of these guys, and the first time I've seen them smile. They don't get along with the superior officers, and they could just about spit on us privates, but now I'm suddenly getting the benefit of McClean's vast wisdom and insight. Something ain't right.

Maybe I was wrong. Maybe we actually were ambushed back there and killed. Maybe this is death.

"Well," I tell him, "I guess I'm doing it righter than I thought, because so far I'm killing nothing but time here. But I'm really slaughtering that."

"Ha," he says. "Don't you worry about that part. Enemy kills practically throw themselves in your path sooner or later around here. Then once you've got that out of the way, you can relax and enjoy yourself."

Somehow, that doesn't sound at all like the way it should go.

"Thanks, corporal," I say. "I'll look forward to that."

"That's the spirit," he says.

We march in mostly silence for another mile, then another mile. Not sure about the rest of them, but I know I'm now in a state of total readiness. I'd even dare to say no Girl Scouts will be killing me today. I'd even dare to say that if they tried I might be man enough to wipe out a whole troop of them.

"Hold up," Cpl. McClean says in a hard whisper. He pushes me down into a crouch, goes down himself, and gestures for all the men behind us to get down as well. We have our eyes and ears and weapons trained on the jungle, thick on our right. He taps me on the shoulder and tugs at me to accompany him into the bush. He signals for the rest to stay in position, covering us.

I'm shaking, suddenly sweating sheets of perspiration as we step lightly, silently along what is almost a path but not quite. We're about thirty yards in, and it's getting really thick, and the bugs are eating the flesh right off me. McClean signals a point just ahead where he and I are to split in two directions.

Now, I'm really moisturized. I feel worse than when I was drafted and peed my pants, because at least then there wasn't an immediate threat to my life in addition to the soggy pants.

But I go. I am a soldier. I am a United States Marine and I follow orders and I am here to terrorize the enemy and not to be terrorized by him and if I turned away from this now my pal Ivan would shoot me dead and I'd thank him for it.

"There! There!" McClean screams, and for a second I don't see a thing, other than the whole landscape shaking from my own fear. But then, there he is. I just about step on him before he jumps up, this VC guy, practically right into my face, practically smashing into my face with his own when he jumps up out of the leaf cover and I have to react, just like I've been trained to.

I stick my bayonet right into the guy's gut. He is staring at me, right there, his eyes so wide and his mouth so open. He's holding a rifle, but holding it really weird like his hands are glued together in the middle of the gun, like nobody ever bothered to even tell him the right way to hold it. Poor guy.

But too bad, poor guy. I pull the blade out of him and stick it right back in. Then again and again and again and again. It's something like a sawing motion, very close to a sawing motion, only the blade comes all the way out and back in again, so maybe the action is more like a sewing machine like my mom's, only giant and lethal.

And my mom's machine wouldn't practically take the guy's whole insides and bring them to the outside, like I'm doing.

My mom's *other* machine is what I am now. Mom's killing machine.

The guy falls backward, falls right off my blade onto the seat of his bloody pants because, man, there is blood everywhere. He sits there just soaking in it, soaking and oozing and covering his belly as if he can still hold it all together, hold it all in, which, stupid as I am, even I would never think.

He's looking up at me, and I'm looking down at him. This is one tough, tough doomed dude, I'm thinking as I look at him. I can't see anything in his face really, because I have to admit I have trouble reading these guys' faces, but I know what we have in common is that he was here to kill me and I was here to kill him and so I win.

The other thing we have in common for just these few seconds is the blood. I can see the way the blood is pumping out of him, pulsing in small waves while his heart tries to the end to do its job. Good heart, VC man, good heart. And the pulsing is in exact, exact rhythm with my own blood, pulsing *puh-puh-puh-puh* in my ears and eyes and fingers and neck, so hard I might start oozing all over the place too, so hard it's breaking like waves in my ears, like it might come rushing right on out my ears.

Then the guys are all gathered around behind me, and they're chanting my name, not roaring but whisper-chanting, dangerous jungle style.

"Ruu-dee, Ruu-dee, Ruu-dee . . ."

And it all gets right inside me, cranking me up higher.

And I do it, do it up higher.

I do it again, but I go for the neck. I lunge at my enemy, stick my bayonet in just below his ear, and I pump and stab and see and saw until this is like nothing I've ever seen, like nobody anywhere has ever seen, more blood than there is anywhere, and my enemy, my victory, is propped up almost sitting-like against a tree and almost without the head that he had before he met me.

Eventually, the chanting stops. Everything stops, except my mad mental blood pressure which feels to me like it's thumping the ground and rustling the trees all around.

"Let's move out," Cpl. McClean says kind of solemn-like.

I look back at the faces around me and I think I've done something here, because these are not the faces I ever saw before. I did something. Scared people. Impressed people. Shocked and awed and somethinged people, but I changed them, that's for sure, and while I never know anything, right this minute I sure know something, and that is that things have *changed*. Right now. Inside and out.

I wish for all the world that Ivan was here now. That's what I'm wishing most, right at this big, big-change minute of my life.

"I'll be right behind you, corporal," I say quietly, through heavy, fast breath that I fight to control.

He does a bit of a double-take, but just a bit. Then he nods. "Five minutes, private," he says to me. "We can't be leaving you behind. Not even you. So you catch up to us in five minutes. That's an order."

I can take an order. Any order, any degree of difficulty, any time, I can take an order. I am a United States Marine.

"Yes, sir."

When the men are just far enough away, I sit. I sit right down, in the pond of blood, next to my defeated enemy soldier, my first confirmed kill that should probably count as more than one because I killed him so much.

"Sorry," I say to him. "And thank you."

I make a joke to him, asking for my "you're welcome." And when I don't get it I question his manners and ask him if he was raised in a barn, because that's what my mother always said to rudeness. I say it because I guess I'm hoping a joke will make my hands stop shaking. It doesn't.

"Well, I'm gonna have to leave you, soldier," I say, rolling forward onto my knees. "And sorry, but I'll be taking this weapon."

It's what you do. No disrespect, it's just what you do.

I go to remove the rifle, which is still, amazingly, in that awkward grip of his.

And more amazingly, it won't come. I tug again, and his slick purple-red hands move with it. That freaks me out a bit, so I pull my hand away. Then, slowly and gently, I reach in again and raise the gun up.

And I see. His hands come up with the weapon, because they're secured to the weapon. They're tied, strapped with wire, to the gun. The kind of wire they use to bind prisoners' hands. Then I look down to his bare feet. Which are also bound together with wire, and the wire connected to the tree five feet away.

He wasn't a real fighter. At least not by the time I met him. He was fodder. Like one of those poor sap goats that villagers will tie up to lure a rogue tiger.

It was all set up.

For me.

I do catch up, within the five minutes, just as ordered. I fall into line at the back, and I'm blowing air because I had to run to make it, so my arrival is not quite the stealthy silent Marine progress we like to make in the jungle. They must know I'm right behind them.

But you'd think they didn't. Not a single head turns, not a voice speaks. The guys just walk on as if they don't notice me or anything special at all about what happened.

I notice. Drums are beating in my head. They beat-beat-beat just as sure as if we were marching with a military band escort, only the drums beating aren't those crisp and strict ones like you hear at parades. They're wild things, tribal things, and they're making my head hurt and getting louder-louder. I notice it's the feet. The feet, boots on the ground, the pounding and marching of the men in front of me is making the drums wail and my skull is cracking with it and it's the heat, too. And I'm sweating now as if I'm a candy apple, I'm dipped in hot caramel, or whatever that red stuff is that they dip the candy apples in but I feel like I'm just exactly that, that apple at exactly that moment when it's dipped. In the burning hot melted candy.

And it stings my eyes and it's the sweat. And the blood. Of course. I look at my hands while the boot stomps are cracking my candy apple head. I'm absolutely covered in that guy's blood. Covered in it. Covered in it and it's melting down all over me from my head right on down over me and it's sticky and thick in the heat. But I could be convinced, with the look of it and the way everything feels, that it's actually seeping out of me, out of the cracks in my skull.

"Are you with us, Cabbage?" It's Hunter. He's slowed way down because apparently I've slowed way down, and the United States Marine Corps never leaves a man behind. Hunter is leaning close to my face. To the awfulness that my bloody face must be.

"I'm with us," I say. "Sure, I'm with us."

Hunter's all right. Hunter's a good guy and I like him.

"You sure you're okay?"

"Of course. What do you think?"

"Okay, then congratulations, I guess. First confirmed kill."

I feel the blood uncake on my lips when I smile. "Confirmed? You think?"

At first I see Hunter pull his face away from me. He has his hand on my back, I now notice, pushing my speed a little. We've definitely dropped off the pace. He's looking at me in a weird, trying-to-figure-it-out kind of way.

Then his face relaxes, and he pats my back. "Uh, yeah, I'd say we can confirm the kill. I can never keep track of the religions they got all over the place here, but if that guy believed in reincarnation then I think you snuffed out his next life and the one after that, too."

"Good for me," I say. It comes out just as stupid as it sounds.

"Who's Ivan?" Hunter asks as we near the back of the pack again.

"What?" He freaks me out a little with this.

"Ivan. Before you dropped back I was listening to you whispering and growling and muttering stuff to somebody named Ivan."

I push Hunter's hand off my back, march a little more quickly so that I reach the company just before he does and he has to bring up the rear now. I'm not going to be last anymore.

I'm not going to be last ever, anymore.

"Ivan's my brother," I say, even though 'til now I've always been an only child. "He's a killer, just like me. We're killer brothers."

"Well, Ivan would be proud of ya, Cabbage."

"He would be, you're right," I say. "He would, and he will."

PART
TWO

CHAPTER FIVE

Dedicated to Ivan

I hate writing letters. I look at the writing after I've done it and I feel like the stupidest guy ever. I can't help thinking a guy who writes like that should not be allowed to cross the street by himself.

Good thing there are pretty much no streets around here.

And I *have* to write. After the war I might never do it again, but I have to be in contact with certain people right now or it's worse even than being dead.

Brother Ivan,

Some days here everything surprises you. Some days nothing does. Have you noticed that? Well no because nothing ever surprises you because you are always ready for everything, right, and if you're not ready for it then it's probably worse for the surprise than it is for you.

I'm almost like your equal now so what do you think of that?

See, because this is a letter and not a face-to-face I can tell you that and not be scared that you are going to murder me. I should have wrote to you all the time back home, would of saved me a lot of beatings right? Ha ha.

But you know what? It's almost like I am not scared. Of anything. Even you.

Do you feel like you could do just anything here, Ivan? I mean more than even before since you could always do whatever you wanted to? I mean, do you feel like you could do whatever not just because there seems to be no laws here but also because you just feel it? Feel it, I mean. That you could do anything if you needed to. Or even if you didn't need to you could do it anyway? Do you know what I mean? You know what I mean. I don't know if Morris would know what I mean and I am surely sure Beck wouldn't know what I mean but I think you know what I mean.

You would be proud of me here, Ivan. You would be so proud of me that I am proud just thinking about how proud of me you would be. Does that make sense? Doesn't matter, right because things don't have to make sense here.

Except it does. It all does. Everything here

has started to make sense to me. More than anything ever did anywhere. And I owe all that to you. I owe all that I am to you. I might be in Canada if it wasn't for you you know that? Of course you know that. Only you know and I know certain stuff isn't that right Ivan?

I dedicated one to you, buddy. A kill. Just so you know. I bet nobody ever did that for you before I bet that. I just thought of it, it came into my head and it was right. For Ivan, I said, to Ivan. Like you are a god. Like you are. How does that feel? Well there is more where that came from. Lots and lots and lots more cause I feel like I could kill this whole country by myself if I got the order to. I am great at that. I have never been great at anything almost never even been pretty good at anything but I am great great great at taking orders no matter what they are. But don't worry I will leave some for you.

Some guys here are no good at taking orders and I hate that. I can't stand or understand that. Don't you hate that?

I'm different you know. You wouldn't recognize me. I am so different a man now and I am never going back. And I am gonna keep paying you back for this for all you done for all you made of me.

Be proud of me okay? Just do that.

Your brother,
Rudi

I have three excellent guys I spend a lot of my time with. Squid and Hunter and Marquette are guys you'd almost want to spend time with even if you didn't need them covering your back with an M-16 every time you went to the bathroom. Gillespie, I don't know about. He's mostly okay, but I get a feeling from him that's different. He's even worse about rules than the rest of them — and that's pretty bad. Can't stand to follow orders. Or maybe he's just selective about who he wants giving them out, which makes Marine life sort of complicated. He thinks everybody above the rank of corporal is as dangerous as the enemy. And whenever you talk to him he smiles, really hard and constant, and it never feels like a smile at all. That's probably the part I don't like most. I would feel a lot better about him if he just let his face tell the truth instead of doing all that grinning. His nickname is Sunshine, but not when he's around to hear it.

But he's all right, Gillespie. As far as guys go. The way I hear it, we're pretty lucky, at this point in the war, at this spot in-country, that we aren't surrounded by Americans who all want to kill each other. You know how it is when it's really hot in the city for a long time in the summer? How everybody gets on everybody else's nerves and the crime rate goes up and all that? That's what it's like here. Only everybody's armed to the teeth, and it's hotter than wherever else you could be.

But we don't have it all bad at this spot at this time. Chu Lai actually has one of the nicest beaches I've ever seen. And when it's face-melt hot, there's nothing like the beach.

"Maybe if the man could give you the feeling that he knew what he was doing, it would be different." Marquette is talking. He's leading our little formation as we hit the last part of the road before the sand. It is a little bit comical, our formation. We take our guns with us everywhere, of course, but otherwise, we are traveling light. Except for our boxer shorts, we are a formation of nearly naked guys, with guns slung over our shoulders. It is a beach trip, after all.

"Jupp is worse than useless," Gillespie pipes up. "I don't know what he's even doing here."

"Killing time, man," Hunter says. "Just like everybody else."

"No," Gillespie says. "No, no, not like everybody else. Not like me. Not like ol' Cabbage here. *We* keep getting sent into that jungle and all them creepy little villages and killing everybody like they tell us to and getting shot at. But Jupp, man, he never goes nowhere. Never. He just orders and directs and shouts and assigns. Then he shrinks back into his hooch until it's time for chow."

We have reached the beach, and we don't break stride. Guns and all, the five of us march right down over the burning sand and straight into the surf, where we continue the discussion in waist-high water.

"Who's got the soap?" Squid asks. This is also a hygiene trip.

Marquette whips the new bar of soap at Squid. It bounces off his chest and falls under the water. We don't have the floaty kind of soap, so Squid has to dive right under after it.

"Good thing he's a sea creature," Hunter says.

"And how 'bout those corporals?" Marquette says, and now it's pretty clearly become a game of how furious can we get Sunshine.

Sunshine doesn't let us down.

"Slugs!" he shouts, punching the ocean hard enough to send Squid shooting up out of it like he's performing at the aquarium or something. "Those guys . . . it's like they aren't even here as part of the Marines. Like they're on some kind of separate contract working for some other operation altogether. It's like they're self-employed."

"At least they go out," I say. "They go into the jungle and do stuff sometimes."

"Yeah, when they feel like it," Gillespie says.

"Yeah," Hunter says, "but they do feel like it from time to time. Not like the lieutenant."

They won't let Sunshine relax today. This seems kind of dangerous, and I take a plunge underwater when I see his head go all purple.

"— if they would let me!" he's screaming when I come back up. The other guys are laughing, and the way the one bar of soap is being tossed around, this feels — really, really weirdly — like one of the more social gatherings I've been at here. Nobody even looks up as a helicopter from the base *thup-thup*s past above us, drowning out Gillespie's rant. Well, almost drowning it out.

One by one we all get cleaned up and cooled off and one by one we migrate out of the water and up to the beach. I see Hunter up there, making snow angels in the sand, which I suppose should be called sand angels.

"Almost over anyway," Marquette says, catching up to me in the shallows.

"Huh?"

"This," he says, gesturing at Vietnam. "There's not much left of it. You can feel it. Nobody's really even trying anymore because everybody knows we're wasting our time. These third-world peons are making us look stupid. If I was Jupp, I'd stay in my bed all the time, too. Not because I'm a lazy coward like him, but because I'm too smart to waste my time and maybe my life on a war that nobody but a moron thinks that we might win at this point."

I keep walking, splashing, then padding on the wet sand that goes from cool to hot in three steps.

"*I'm* trying," I say, working in more ways than one to be cool. "I'm trying, like I've always been trying, like I'm gonna keep on trying until somebody tells me it's over. And yeah, I believe we can win."

Funny enough, Private Marquette of the United States Marine Corps seems unimpressed by my statement of dedication to the cause. In fact, he seems kind of irritated.

"Good for you, Cabbage. Good for you, hero."

I keep walking toward the angel. Behind us, Gillespie is still raving to Squid about the military command structure.

"Is there something wrong with that?" I say to Marquette, and I have to admit this is the angriest I've been at any time in Vietnam. Even when I killed somebody, I wasn't this angry.

"No, nothing wrong with that at all, Cabbage." I

don't like my nickname right now. For the first time, the way he's saying it, I don't like it at all.

"Good," I say, and I say it strong because I feel like I accomplished something there.

"I mean, *somebody's* got to kill all those dangerous, unarmed, bound-up little prisoners for us. You keep up the good work, and we'll all sleep better."

Controlled fury. That is what a Marine is supposed to harness. He is not supposed to lose control of his emotions because that's when he makes bad decisions.

I am a Marine. I am a very good Marine.

"I killed an enemy soldier."

He laughs at me, the kind of laugh with spit in it. That's not supposed to happen anymore. I'm not in Boston anymore. I am a Marine. They're not supposed to laugh like that.

"You killed a piñata," he says.

I have my M-16 over my shoulder, like always. Usually, it just hangs against my back and I hardly know it's there. But now, I feel it. Now, I know it's there. I'm reaching behind me, feeling for it, gripping it.

"I am a US Marine," I say. "Which I guess is more than I can say for you."

He laughs again. He has to stop doing that. He has to.

"You are a US joke," he says.

Of all the things that have happened to me, from the fright of my induction notice to the punishment of boot camp, to the shooting and the heat and the killing of the war, nothing has knocked me as sideways as I feel right this minute.

Fourth grade. Fourth grade, second time. That was when I got to know my friends, my guys, Morris and Beck and especially Ivan. They showed up like angels — tough angels — right when I needed them. These two fifth-grade idiots, Arthur and Teddy, had me on my knees. On my knees in the gutter of Moraine Street among all the stuff from my book bag. They'd dumped all of it out — books, pencils, an oversize eraser that I got from the science museum, and half of a tuna-and-potato-chips sandwich that I was saving for cartoons when I got home 'cause there probably wasn't much else there. Only now it was stepped on.

I was praying. I was praying with my hands folded and my knees hurting from pebbles. Arthur and Teddy were forcing me to pray, because that's the kind of thing that made them happy and I was the kind of guy that asked for it.

Only when I prayed this time, it worked. They showed up. Like angels. And some people don't believe in that kind of stuff, but I do — or I did, from the time those guys answered my prayer. Ivan and Beck and

Morris chased those jerks away and let them know I was not to be their whipping boy ever again, and that was how we came together forever.

Only they aren't here now. And I suddenly feel like I'm on my knees on Moraine Street.

I'm startled when I feel a quick, hard grip on my hand. I look down, where I had half swung my rifle around front without even realizing it. On my hand, on the gun, I see Gillespie's hand. I turn to see him staring hard at me, but talking to Marquette, all as we keep walking up the beach.

"Marquette, man," Gillespie says, "why don't you just do your own war your own way and leave Cabbage to do his his way. Right?"

Marquette looks sideways at Gillespie. It feels tense, but he doesn't say anything.

"Hey, I can do one of those," Squid says as we come up on Hunter, who is now admiring his sand angel. Squid throws himself down next to it and begins flapping madly, with his gun at his side.

Angels with guns. That seems kind of right to me.

I throw myself down on the other side of Hunter's angel and flap away with my arms and legs until I believe I have made a proper impression.

I hop up. Squid keeps pumping, like he wants to

indent himself deep enough for the folks at home to see it in the other side of the world.

"What about you guys?" Hunter says to Gillespie and Marquette.

"I don't think so," Gillespie says. "A Marine in a war zone lying on his back out in the wide open doesn't sound like the sanest proposition."

That appears to have persuaded Marquette, who seems to want to declare the war over right now all by himself. He falls into line with the others, makes his impression, then he and Squid push up off the sand, trying not to disturb their work.

"Arggh," Marquette barks, turning awkwardly and contorting his shoulder as he falls sideways.

Hunter helps him up, and it's obvious that he's done some damage to his shoulder. Gillespie laughs, a little low and cruel. Enough to get his message across. Then he leads the march back toward camp.

Squid follows, then Marquette pretending hard not to be favoring his other shoulder, then Hunter. I linger a few ticks, admiring our sand work. I feel something good about our armed angels, about leaving our mark on the Chu Lai beach.

And the fact that Marquette actually injured himself in this dangerous operation doesn't hurt, either.

CHAPTER SIX

Brute Force in a Can

Gentlemen, we got work to do," says Cpl. Cherry.

It is first thing in the morning, which is not quite as first thing as first thing used to be. It seems every week we are allowed to sleep in a little later if we feel like it, and if the heat lets us, and if the insects don't become such whining, buzzing little alarm clocks that staying in bed is no treat at all.

"What kind of work?" asks Hunter, up on his elbows on his bunk. "I hope it's not another . . . hold on, did you say *we*?"

"Yes I did, and what's wrong with that?"

One by one the guys are rising on their bunks, like a pod of prairie dogs with a coyote on the horizon.

"Nothing's *wrong* with it, exactly. It's just that you don't seem all that interested in going out on patrols much."

"Well maybe that's because we don't go out on sure-thing search and destroys much."

"What?" Gillespie says, hopping right up and jumping just about straight into his pants.

"That's right, kids: Search. And. Destroy. The kind of mission the big guys get."

And just like that, the whole hooch is transformed. We were a whole lot more House of Reptiles before the news, like a bunch of lizards basking on hot rocks. Now, it's the House of Speed, everybody dressing, pulling on gear, arming up.

"Stop that," Hunter says, slapping my deodorant out of my hand. "Who do you need to smell pretty for anyway?"

"I don't know," I say. "You? To be honest, you've all been starting to get pretty rank smelling around here."

"Well if you don't want to get pretty *dead* smelling, you better leave that deodorant right out of the equation. Charlie can smell that from a mile away."

I turn to Cpl. Cherry, who is still standing in the doorway like he's in charge of supervising dress-up time.

"It's true, Cabbage," he says. "And you better hope your soap isn't too perfumey, either. The hunter becomes the prey pretty quickly in this jungle."

"Hey!" yells Hunter.

Everybody is laughing now.

It's weird. I realize this. We're as happy as a bunch of school kids on a field-trip day. Morale, which is something we hear discussed a great deal lately, seems to have been repaired with that one phrase: *search and destroy.*

It is a whole different thing, the search-and-destroy mission. It means we have intelligence about an enemy installation — we know where they are, and we are supposed to ride in and blow the daylights out of them. It is the opposite of the scouting patrols that once made up the bulk of our duties. On those, there was the overwhelming feeling that, honestly, we were there as much to attract enemy fire as we were to do any real scouting. Because when somebody shoots at you, they tend to give their position away. It isn't a very comforting feeling.

Not that getting our guys shot up and blown up and all that was ever the plan, but the Marines are the Marines and we would do whatever it took to get the job accomplished, even if it cost lives.

Somebody up top stopped feeling that way at some point. Word came down, and the word was: no more casualties. And so we've been getting more cautious.

But while we don't want to absorb any more casualties, nobody said anything about dishing out any less. In fact, body counts are the way we are keeping score now, and that too has come down from way up. And places where we used to have to go on tiptoe and try not to upset the locals even when the locals already wanted our scalps, well, a lot of those places have been designated free-fire zones now.

I get goose bumps just thinking that in my head. *Free-fire zones.*

Just like search and destroy, free-fire zones are just what they sound like they are — fire freely, gentlemen, fire freely.

"Well?" Cpl. McClean says, poking his head in the door behind Cherry. "Everybody tooled up?"

Barks. Woofs and howls and yips and every other animal noise our talents will allow are the answers to that question.

"Good, because our ride is here, and the lieutenant is rarin' to go."

All noise stops as quick as if somebody lifted the needle off the record.

"The *who* is rarin' to *what*?" says Marquette.

McClean gets a big, mean grin across his face. "That's right, soldiers. This is an *important* mission."

Marquette claps his hands loudly once, then again, then rubs them together. "You mean this is an *easy* mission," he says, and everybody breaks up laughing.

Sorry, that would be *almost* everybody.

"So you don't need me, then," Squid says, lying back down on his bunk half-dressed.

"Everybody!" Cpl. Cherry barks. "We expect to see every one of you outside in ten minutes, ready to saddle up."

As the two corporals head on out, Squid just lies motionless.

I make my way over to his bunk, crouch down beside him. I feel Hunter hovering over my shoulder while the other guys go on as if nothing is the matter.

"What are you doing, man?" I ask Squid.

"Sleeping this one out," he says.

"You can't do that," I say.

"I'm gonna try."

"What's the matter with you?" Hunter says.

"I thought this was all over," Squid says. "We haven't been doing nothing. I liked it. I told my dad it was over. I only got a month left, and I know how this stuff works. We see no action for ages, then I stick my head out there and get it shot off, just in time to go home. Just like the movies."

"It's not like the movies," I say. "Nothing here is anything like any movie I ever saw."

"Shut up already," Marquette says. "Let him stay if he's gonna be like that. We don't need him."

"I only got a month left. I don't want to search and destroy nothin'. I only got a month left, guys."

"Yeah," I say, "I think you mentioned that."

"I want to see my dad."

I mentioned that Squid is a good guy. He is probably the guy who is liked best in the squad, mostly because he never does a thing that anybody could get bothered about. He has never balked at an order, a request, a suggestion, even.

Not 'til now.

"Get up, Squid," I say.

"Easy, Cabbage," Hunter says, putting a hand on my shoulder.

"Leave him there," Marquette says. It's not that he's siding with Squid. He just doesn't care. He is out the door with a slam.

"Get up, Squid," I say.

"Listen, Squid," Hunter says. "Did you hear that even Jupp is coming with us? You know what that means?"

"It means he's gonna order me to go, and I don't care."

"No, it means if he's out there with us this mission must be such a sure thing that you'll be in more danger here on your bunk than out there with us."

Gillespie laughs out loud at that.

I can't laugh right now. It's a good line, but it ain't funny.

"You and your dad can be whatever you want to be a month from now," I say, leaning maybe a little too close to Squid's face. "But right this minute you are a United States Marine. And you have received an order. We follow orders."

He just lies there, staring up at me with his scaredy eyes and his stupid squid-shaped skull.

"You can do this," I say.

He attempts to roll over, away from me.

Like a cobra, I react, snagging him by the tee shirt with both hands and pulling him around my way.

I feel Hunter's hand let go of my shoulder.

"Hunter," Squid says, kind of sad, kind of desperate, kind of infuriating. I hear the door slap shut and know Hunter's left.

"Gillespie," Squid pleads, proving just how desperate he is.

"The man's right, Squid," Gillespie says, the door squealing open again. "You are a Marine, man."

We're alone now, and the pathetic look on Squid's face is making me demented. I find myself staring at him hard, staring into his eyes. I get close to his face again, trying to, I don't know, smell what's inside him? I pull him still closer, and I see how afraid he is — really honestly afraid.

Of war.

Of not seeing his dad again.

Of *me*.

How far have I come, from home, from that life?

I get this surge of power, of strength, of rage at Squid's weakness, and I think: How awful to be like that. How sickening.

"What would Ivan say to this?" I scream in his face, practically spitting on him. His features fold up into that pre-cry scrunch, and that is beyond the last straw.

Smack. I slap poor decent Squid right across the face.

Just like I was General Patton or something.

Then I drag him out of his bunk, over to his locker. I pull a fresh shirt out and start wrestling it right onto him.

"All right," he says, his voice cracking but somehow at the same time strong. "All right, all right," he says, then, catching me totally by surprise, he blasts me right in the chest with an explosive two-handed shove that sends me backward, into and over Gillespie's bunk and onto the floor.

When I get up, he is buttoning his shirt about as aggressively as a person can do that and looking at me with blood in his eyes. I am on my knees at the side of Gillespie's bunk like I am saying my bedtime prayers.

"Guess I'll see you outside, then," I say.

He just glares at me, continues suiting up, and I head out.

When I get outside, I see my guys about fifty yards away, piling into the rear of an M-113 armored troop carrier. This machine is usually part of the Army's gear but more and more are being turned over to the South Vietnamese forces, the ARVN. We are working with our foreign allies today.

I hurry to catch up, and when I reach the vehicle I get a kind of rush of excitement since I've never been in one before. It's something between a truck and a tank, with all the armor plating made of aluminum to keep it light and fast. The corporals are standing like security guards at each side of the open back of the vehicle, and sitting up top manning the machine gun is an ARVN soldier. The door at the back is bottom-hinge, open and waiting for me like a small up ramp onto the expressway.

Lt. Jupp is standing at the entrance like a greeter, or like he owns the thing personally. He is smiling at me. "Ready for the big time, Cabbage?"

"Yes, sir," I say.

I stand at the back, looking in before I mount the ramp. The guys on my fire team are inside, sitting, lined up on benches mounted along each wall. Everywhere else, floor to ceiling, under the benches and against the walls, firepower is packed and stacked. There looks to be enough artillery in this vehicle for each man on board to take out a small city himself. I don't even want to think about what would happen if a rocket somehow hit this rolling munitions depot.

We have mortar and 3.5-inch rocket launchers. We have Claymore anti-personnel mines and M-60 machine guns, M-79 grenade launchers, and — from what I can read on the sides of the crates toward the back under the benches — every type of grenade from white phosphorus to fragmentation and beehive shells that sound like gigantic murder bees when they come shooting out of the launcher.

I must be staring stupid at it all because next thing I know Cpl. Cherry is snapping his fingers in front of my face, and everybody laughs out loud.

"Right!" Lt. Jupp bellows like he likes to. "Is everyone here? Time to move out!"

The rest of us have all boarded the vehicle, squeezed in on the benches. The ARVN driver has started it up. And we all look back in the direction of our hooch.

"Well?" Lt. Jupp barks, about to climb up.

Come on, Squid, man. Come on.

"Come on," Hunter says, low but audible. "Come on. . . ."

Jupp is up. He's about to close the back door.

Then Squid comes barreling out of the hooch, still pulling his clothes and his gear all together, like he just made the decision ten seconds ago.

"Squiiiiid!" Hunter yells, and all the guys whoop and cheer and hoot at him as he runs to catch up and finally just tumbles into the back of the vehicle, where Sunshine and I pull him all the way in and the trap is shut and we are on our way to the action.

"What a stink wagon!" Marquette yells almost as soon as the door is pulled up. "Man, this is a stench."

He could not be more right about this. I mean, these guys smell. They — and I suppose possibly me — always smell. But now we're sealed up in a small space, rolling along at a good clip — top speed for this machine is about forty miles per hour, which is pretty much *flying* for a tanklike beast — and bouncing all around and into each other. We're laughing and roaring and reeking, in a way that hasn't happened before. I don't quite recognize it.

"The testosterone in this thing is thick enough to cut with a bayonet," Jupp declares.

"I tried to put on deodorant," I say, "but I wasn't allowed."

"That would do you no good now, Cabbage," he says, bellow-laughing. Lt. Jupp's loudness is magnified, a lot, inside these aluminum walls. But for the moment and for once nobody seems bothered. "Jeez, if somebody lights a match in here we're all barbecued."

I laugh along with everybody else, even as I am thinking about what I heard about the M-113. That despite the armor and the speed and all, with the fuel tank built right below where we're sitting, we're vulnerable. If we run over a land mine we will indeed be fried alive.

I'm surely not the only one who knows about that and I am just as surely not the only one who doesn't care. We are achieving something really unusual in my so-far limited wartime experience: a united sense of purpose. Nobody's telling us we can't win. Nobody's telling us to back off or lay low or stay in bed. We're going to the action and we're going guns a' blazin', and it might not last long but as of now this unit of the USMC has got *Semper Fi* spirit and God help whoever gets in our way today.

We're brute force in a can.

But it's like Squid isn't on the same wavelength. He's sitting across from me, looking down as Lt. Jupp fills us in some.

"Right, men, here's the story. There is a nest of trouble about thirty miles west of us, a village that's been rumbled twice already by the ARVN, only to have the whole thing restaffed in less than a week both times. It's a depot for VC arms and guerillas and communications and the works. Not a sprawling operation, but a serious nuisance. And since the local army has been unable — or unwilling — to stamp out this little nest properly, the brass have called in the professionals, with explicit instructions to wipe this threat out *by any means necessary*." As he says this phrase Jupp makes a sweeping gesture, like he is a museum tour guide showing us the Implements of Death exhibit.

The crowd goes mental again.

But Squid keeps looking down at the floor. I motion across to Gillespie, who's sitting next to him, and get him to switch seats with me.

"You okay?" I ask Squid, staring down at the same spot between his feet.

"Fine," he says.

"Sorry," I say. "About smacking you and all. It's just that —"

"You did the right thing. Shut up."

"Thanks for saying that."

"No sweat. Here's another one for ya: Shut up."

I laugh, and he makes a noise that I think might qualify as laughing along.

"Are you scared?" I ask, as we hit a bump that could well have been a buffalo and throws us all up and down across the floor and each other.

"Of course I'm scared," he says as we re-take our seats. "Been scared every single day since I got here. But it got better, got routine. Then it got quiet. The quiet, Rudi . . ."

The odd occasion when I hear my name makes me, just a tiny bit and just for a half second, choke up. Stupid.

". . . the quiet, it went and did something to my head. I'd gotten used to things, but then once we got to the quiet part, it was like I could hear, almost, a ticking in my head. I became so aware of the clock and the calendar and my DEROS, and I thought about being a short-timer and almost home, and instead of making me feel good, it made me petrified I wasn't gonna *get* home. I need to see my dad. That's all I can think about. He's alone. I just gotta get home. And everything was going okay, looked like we were out of the game, and I loved that. And then . . ."

"And then this," I say, understanding a little better.

"And then *this*," he says, moving his hands from his lap, revealing a pretty good stain of wet.

"Pffftt!" I sputter, laughing without meaning to.

He quickly covers up again, with his helmet this time, and crosses his legs. His sad squid head is exposed now, and it's gone all red. "Thanks, jerk," he says. "I was hoping you would understand." He turns his head away.

"I do," I say, still laughing a little as I lean right up to his red ear and tell him how I oh-so-courageously peed myself at my induction letter.

"Really?" he says, laughing now along with everybody else. It is a strange thing, no question about it: Every man on board is laughing at something or other that's been said by another man, and if you stopped the vehicle and climbed in you would think this was the tightest team of fighting men ever assembled. Like we all get along and work together in well-oiled and smelly government-issue harmony.

That's the power of search and destroy, I guess.

"Stick close to me," I say, suddenly feeling like the big brother for once. "I will make sure nothing stands between you and seeing your dad, okay?"

He turns and, grinning like a monkey, gets his face right up close to mine. He puts his pee-essence helmet back on and, jeez, he looks for a flash so much like an ol' Rudy-Judy that I want to shove him right off this armored transport and leave him for dead, leave him for the Vietcong and for the rats and fire ants and leeches that rule this awful jungle.

I can tell by the incline that we are making our way up a steepish hill, which means we are nearing our destination. There is an NZ, that's a landing zone, on a rise overlooking this village we will be clobbering. So if we need to call in support even that will be available to us. But Lt. Jupp sounds so confident about everything, I almost feel embarrassed we didn't leave a couple guys behind.

"There is nowhere for these people to run to the west of here because the ARVN troops have them all pinned in on that side. And we have everything cleared between here and the rise overlooking the village. All there is for us to do is to bring down the heavy rain on them, then when the deed is done follow on down and see that the site is secured. But we need to make visual contact first, confirm the intelligence, so that when we begin free-fire, we know what we are going after. That is why this has to be a ground operation. Understood?"

"Yessir," we say, one after another. "Yessir yes —"

Bu-hoom!

"Holy smokes!" Gillespie shouts.

The whole vehicle has jumped up and come bouncing down again. Some kind of medium artillery has gone off close enough to raise the whole twelve tons of us right up off the earth.

Bu-hoom!

It happens again. The ARVN driver is shouting to his gunner up top in Vietnamese, and the gunner starts blasting off round after round into the surrounding area while we keep hurtling on. Somebody out there returns equal fire, machine-gun rounds pinging off the aluminum armor with enough frequency that they could be right outside smacking us with golf irons.

The big door is getting drummed with thousands of shots.

They're behind us.

"I thought you said this was all clear?" Cpl. Cherry shouts at Lt. Jupp.

"It was!" Jupp shouts back.

Ping-ping-ping-ping-ping. It's like an arcade game at Paragon Park.

"They don't agree!" Marquette screams.

The driver is yelling in Vietnamese and a bit of English at Lt. Jupp, who shouts back at him. "Drive, Lieutenant Bien! Just go. Just keep going!"

He's not just a driver. He's a lieutenant in the ARVN, with a name and everything. Why should this be news?

You don't have to understand Vietnamese to know that Lt. Bien is livid. He goes up a couple of octaves as he screams himself mental at the other lieutenant. Up top, the gunner — who I now imagine also has a name we don't know — is a hero, blasting away in his one-man war against however many of whoever is out there.

Lt. Bien maneuvers this way and that, throwing us around like GI Joe dolls, finally swooping down into a ditch and stopping. He screams some more at Jupp.

"Who is in charge here?" Cpl. McClean shouts at Jupp.

"I am," Jupp says.

The words are meaningless. Because he says them with such a complete lack of enthusiasm that I get an instant chill of terror. The bullets continue to riddle the right side of our M-113.

But the return fire above abruptly stops.

Lt. Bien shouts horrors straight up into the air, then pulls a lever that throws open the tailgate.

And we US Marines, hollering like madmen, pile out with our M-16s firing in all directions.

We hit the ground, crawling up to the lip of the crater we'd ditched into. All of the enemy fire appears to be coming from the same general direction.

"Can't be more than a squad, no bigger than ours," Gillespie says. He is actually coordinating, pointing out individual spots along the ridge for guys to spread out to. Nobody questions it. Nobody balks.

It is a plain, old-fashioned firefight, the kind I had come to this country expecting to face pretty much every day. My heart is hitting me so hard that I'm convinced it'll punch away any bullet that hits my chest. You can see the muzzle flash from the Russian AK-47s the VC fighters use. They're no more than a couple hundred yards away.

The closest guy to me is Squid, and he's going completely psycho-squid, like if John Wayne was a sea creature with mental problems and a grudge.

"Arrgh, arrrrgh, arrrgh," he says, spraying bullets like mad into the jungle.

It seems like they're already out of RPGs — the rocket-propelled grenades I assume they were firing at our vehicle before — because we're taking nothing but machine-gun fire at this point.

Then there's a sound.

Sshshshshshshsuuuuuuuuf . . . bu-hooom.

Okay, so I was wrong about the RPGs. That one must have sailed no more than three feet over me, 'cause I felt the back draft of the thing tug at my clothes before it *bu-hoom*ed way back behind us. ARVN Lt. Bien knows his stuff — ditching in this crater probably just saved us our ride. And everything that comes with it.

Like the artillery.

Lt. Bien is right up behind me, patting me on the

back. First I jump, scared nutty, then I turn to see him positioning a rocket launcher on my shoulder. It's an M-67 and is called a recoilless rifle, but nobody's fooled by that. You could rightly call it a bazooka, or a rocket launcher, but I wouldn't call it any kind of rifle.

The lieutenant has another M-67 under his free arm and quickly heads down the line where he gives it to Cpl. Cherry. Cpl. McClean follows right behind with the ammo.

I look to my left to find my assistant, Squid, staring at the bundle of three buzz rockets in his shaking arms.

"Well, you gonna marry 'em, or what?" I say.

"Oh," he says.

"Load!" I snap at him.

He drops behind me, where I've taken up a half-kneeling position another foot or so down from the lip of the crater. I can see out of the corner of my eye as Hunter loads for Cherry, and, *zzzzziiiiip*, *shoom* the rocket goes off, like a rocket. One second later, *boooom!* There's a massive blast right near the muzzle flashes of the enemy nest. Fire burns right up into the sky.

"Come on, man!" I say, and he slaps my shoulder and I fire: *zzziiiip*, *shoooom . . . booom!*

I watch the trees in the distance explode with the rocket's impact, and my heart does things that make it seem like it's been switched off my whole life until right now.

"Come on, man, come on!" I say when I hear Squid fumbling around back there. He shakes and jostles me around, then I hear him snap the breach closed before slapping my shoulder again.

Snap-slap-trigger-*schooooom . . . bu-hooom!*

Man, we can feel the heat of the flames from here as the trees all around Charlie go right up. The rest of the guys keep the pressure on, peppering the scorching air with machine-gun fire until somebody, I think it's Cherry, calls for a halt.

There are still shots coming at us. It seems to be one guy. We can pinpoint the *pop*s of his gun.

"Fire-fire-fire!" Cherry shouts, and Lord have mercy, all our guns pour in on that spot like the greatest threat to the free world is located in that one guy and Cherry fires *his* rocket once more and so, jeez, I won't be left out so *schooooom . . . bu-hoom* I pile on in there and stick a fork in 'em because that nest of birds is cooked and *done.*

I love the M-67 rocket launcher more than a person should love a nonperson.

Cpl. Cherry calls time-out again and everybody stops. I can hear the crackle of fire, the fall of a tree as it crashes to the ground, and nothing else but our own heavy, excited breathing.

That's how the scene remains, for one and two and six minutes, the squad just breathing our total victory in deep until the voice at the far end of our line says, cool but sharp, "Well executed, Marines. Fine work. Now pack up and let's move out."

Every helmeted head on the line turns at once in that direction, toward Lt. Jupp.

"Where were *you*?" Gillespie asks without hiding his disgust even a little.

"I," says Jupp slowly, jungle-low but somehow managing to do his usual shout in there as well, "was right here, where a commander is supposed to be, overseeing operations. And, *private*, I can assure you that is the last time I will be answering to you or anyone else under my command. And I can likewise assure you that if I hear anything like that tone again you *will* be cited for insubordination. Do I make myself clear?"

This, now, is a stare-off. Not just between Jupp and Gillespie. But between Jupp and all the eyes of the squad. How could you look away even if you wanted to?

"I *said*, do I —"

"I heard what you said," says Gillespie, and one by one the starers stop staring. I can't. I want to stop.

Cherry and Hunter and McClean take their M-67 and their shells and selves back to the truck, and Marquette stands and stretches and walks away, and I feel Squid tugging at my sleeve, but I just shrug him off. I want to go. I can't move. I'm stuck to this confrontation.

Until Jupp, looking shiftier and more uncomfortable by the second, looks in my direction. We lock eyes.

He's right, of course. It's not for an enlisted man to question his superior officer — not any time, but especially not out in the field. So I agree with him. No matter what, I have to agree with him, and I do.

Another thing. I don't hate him the way everybody else seems to. I just don't. Sure, he shouts at me all the time. He prefers to stay back instead of going out on patrols. He gives me assignments I'm sometimes not ready for. But so what? I like being shouted at. I like responsibility. I like to be pushed. And if Lt. Jupp isn't the greatest leader in the corps, well, that may be, but judging him isn't my job. My job is to be a good soldier. I am a good soldier.

And right now I don't like what I'm feeling and I don't like the look in my boss's eyes that fails to give me confidence when confidence is pretty darn important.

"Gillespie," I say firmly, and grab him by the back of the shirt. I pull him up lightly from where he has stubbornly remained on the ground. I haul him back in the direction of the armored transport, even though he's bigger than me and stronger than me and smarter than me and — in some way, in some other world — right about what he's doing. I drag him back where he belongs.

And he lets me.

This is such a weird and remarkable day already.

The rest of the run toward our destination is mostly quiet, though *quiet* somehow seems like the wrong word. Nobody's saying much, but you can feel it, the charge in the air, and boy can you smell that stink more than ever. I'm sitting diagonally across from Gillespie, who's looking like he could just jump out of the vehicle unarmed and start biting the heads off all the VC in the area. Lt. Jupp is on the same bench, in the spot up closest to the driver. On Jupp's left is Hunter, who doesn't seem to know him. On his right, curled up on the floor next to the driver, is our dead ARVN gunner, who doesn't know anybody anymore. Cpl. Cherry, who is turning out to be a far more ferocious warrior than I had figured, has taken up the gun post on the roof.

"How you feeling?" I say low to Squid.

"Pretty great, man. I mean, really great. Better than I've felt in a long time. Can't wait now, can't wait."

"I know it," I say. "Let's go, let's go."

Our surviving ARVN comrade is shouting again, as we are apparently approaching our destination. Guys are up and out of their seats, loading up and growling and howling even though the vehicle's still bouncing crazy and we don't even have the head room to stand all the way up so we're a bunch of hunchback gun-toting sweaty smelly lunatics. In a can.

The vehicle jams to a halt, and we all pile out the open rear ramp. Us privates squat right down, followed by the corporals, guns ready, scanning the periphery from our hilltop clearing down over the pretty green countryside below.

Lt. Jupp steps out of the truck but stays in his hunch-back crouch like he isn't quite sure where he is as he studies a map and we all wait. It might be something else or it might be that he was shaken up by Sunshine's mini revolt, but the man doesn't look at all sure of what he's doing.

"Lieutenant," Cpl. McClean snaps. "Have you got coordinates? Have you got a target for us?"

"Yes," Jupp snaps back in that old familiar growl of authority. But he continues studying.

Lt. Bien comes striding out of the M-113, not bothering with the crouching or ducking, and stomps up to the lieutenant as if he has dinner reservations in an hour. He jabs at a point on the map and, not even trying with the English anymore, barks short, stabbing Vietnamese syllables before firmly grasping the lieutenant and turning him in the direction of a barely visible trail of blue smoke coming up out of a dense thicket of canopy about a quarter mile away. As he is pointing, we hear a sound that's becoming pretty familiar.

SSSSSSissssss . . .

And the show's on as a surface-to-air missile comes whizzing right through our party and everybody scrambles. The corporals go for the heavy hardware in the vehicle while we spray mostly ineffective rounds in the direction of the target. I'm half-proud that we're being treated with the same respect as aircraft, but get over that pretty quick when a second SAM comes within five feet of my head.

Soon as it's gone past, though, I start laughing. I know it's truly mental, but I can't help it. It's like the roller coaster at Paragon Park, except without the puking. What I mean is, the anticipation will drive you crazy, but when you survive it, it's a complete thrill. I have adrenaline pumping right out my pores now, and I am chafing for some of that heavy hardware.

I get my wish when McClean comes rushing over and sets me and Squid up with an 81-mm mortar, and it's like basic-training time trials as we get the thing assembled and aimed, packed and loaded in record time. Squid takes a step back and *boom* that shell shoots out and up and higher and higher, arcing over our own Air Force flight patterns and I'll be grilled if I'm not flashing back to Paragon and Nantasket Beach and the Fourth of July fireworks all over again, amazing, until:

Phwooooom! Man, when that shell lands crashing and burning through that canopy I can't believe there's anything in or out of armor that could withstand it.

So we do it again.

And again.

We're absolutely pounding this site, with mortar and heavy cannon fire and RPGs, and I wish they let us have flamethrowers because that's really all that's missing from this celebration. We hit 'em and hit 'em and hit 'em again until the referee would surely stop the fight if this was boxing, but it ain't and so we hit 'em again. Because we are the United States Marine Corps and we are doing, finally, what we were sent here to do. And no offense to the Army of the Republic of South Vietnam, who seem like decent soldiers and swell guys and who have been a lot of help to us today, but there ain't no way in heaven or on earth we're gonna let these guys up off the mat the way they did. Twice. We're gonna make 'em dead and make 'em stay dead regardless of the Vietcong Charlie reputation for coming back like magic. No more magic. None.

And also with all due respect to our brave brothers of the United States Army, the Marines are not a defensive force like they are and we should not ever've been asked to hang around and *defend* any part of this country. We weren't trained for that. We are an offensive force.

"Hold fire! Hold fire!" Lt. Jupp calls out as loud as he can and nobody, but nobody, holds fire right away, not even me. I think he's been calling it out for a while before I even realize he's doing it, to be honest, because my ears are filled with the awesomeness of cannon fire and with my pounding, heaving heart, and truth is if the lieutenant wanted to be heard when he shouted he maybe should be a little more selective about all the shouting he does all the time.

But that's no excuse, really, and when I realize what's what I stop firing well before the other guys do.

I love the 81-mm mortar every bit as much as the M-67 rocket launcher and I hope I never have to choose between the two of them.

It's a little frightening, a little embarrassing to watch Jupp have to go up to one bloodthirsty Marine after another and insist that he stop pummeling whatever is left of the enemy stronghold down there. It's even to the point where he comes scary close to Gillespie's line of fire as he cranes in to shout at him. Gillespie is chuckling like a movie villain and Jupp is leaning harder and harder into him, screaming. I'm pretty sure Gillespie's running out of ammo now is the only thing that saves the lieutenant's life, though not his dignity.

I know how the guys feel. Those enemy guys, whoever they are down there in whatever setup they have going there, have hardly done enough to shake us up too badly. But still, every cell in my body wants to use up every bit of ordnance in our tank to blow them to pieces and blow their pieces to pieces, and those pieces to pieces. They can't be dead enough.

But it's no excuse for ignoring a direct order.

When the men are all finally convinced to stop shooting, we listen.

There is no return fire. No rifle shots, no rockets' red glare. By far the most noticeable noise in this whole soggy, leafy, phospho-smelly patch of jungle is the heavy marathon breathing of Lt. Jupp.

It's hard to tell for sure which is making him hyperventilate like he's doing: the rush of the action or the effort of shouting every one of his men individually into the off position. At any rate, what *is* for sure is that this was not the walk-in-the-park assignment he was expecting it to be.

I have never been more excited in my life.

But I have also never seen Lt. Jupp so tense. His eyes are bugging and bloodshot.

"Is everybody okay?" he says, snarly and shaky both.

There is much gruntage, no words, everybody pretty clearly being okay.

"Once again, superb fighting, men. Job extremely well done. Might have expected you to be rusty from inaction, but you were — to a man — ready, willing, and able, and far too much a match for whoever and whatever was down there. Now, I don't know about you all, but I am ready to get back and get some chow, huh?"

It starts with both corporals. I watch as they go all wide-eyed, their jaws tensing. Then the look makes its way down the chain of command, starting with the more disrespectful privates, Gillespie and Marquette, and passing to Hunter and Squid and, I realize, to me, too. There is genuine shock in these looks. Shock and fury.

"Lieutenant," Cherry says, "we have to go down there."

"We have to follow up," McClean says. "We need to

verify, visually, what we had down there. What was, what is, what we accomplished."

"What might *still* need to be accomplished," Cherry adds.

Jupp, to my disappointment, gives them an unmistakable *are-you-stupid?* look.

"We know what is left to be accomplished, corporal. Nothing. Put your stupid corporal ear to the breeze and listen. We wiped them out. We knocked them into Cambodia and beyond. We did what we were assigned to do, and now our job is to get back. We are lucky to be in one piece, coming home with everybody we brought out with us —"

Gillespie clears his throat loudly as our ally, Lt. Bien, silently turns and walks back to the M-113.

"— and who knows what we are going to engage on the way back? Now, our success today is all well and good, but the very clear directive from all the way up top at this point is *we are not taking any more casualties*. As commanding officer, my number-one priority right now is to get the men under my command back safe, and no matter how cocky you all feel about yourselves right now that is precisely what I intend to do. Now, soldiers, pack up your gear and get yourselves back to that vehicle directly. That is an order."

Lt. Jupp himself starts making a line for the vehicle like he's racing somebody, which isn't the case at all because nobody's moved. He's gone about twenty paces when he senses this is the case. He stops short and, without turning toward us, barks his command again.

"I *said*, that's an order, men."

I don't disobey orders. That's a fact, and that fact isn't going to change as long as I'm a member of the USMC.

But we're supposed to go down and follow up. I know this. Everybody knows this.

We're all looking at the corporals now.

The corporals look at each other.

Cherry shakes his head in disbelief. McClean shrugs. They start heading in the direction of the ride home.

"No!" Gillespie shouts.

"You are sailing very close to the wind, Gillespie," Jupp calls, about to step into the vehicle.

"Just let it go," Cherry says. "It's not worth it."

Despite two firefights, this might be the tensest moment of the day. So far.

We're all headed to the M-113 now, when suddenly our ARVN man hops down and stands nose-to-nose with Lt. Jupp. Jupp freezes, but we all continue to move closer. It's a cozy huddle when Lt. Bien speaks.

"We go down there," he says to Jupp, gesturing in the direction of the bombardment.

We all wait. It's very much like a school yard fight waiting to happen.

But there isn't another word. It's an amazingly tense minute.

We all mount up and move out without another word said.

It is extra bumpy as we hurtle down through the rugged terrain to the site. Bien could well be doing it on purpose, the way he's hunched over the controls and growling lowly in Vietnamese. Lt. Jupp, no question, is a wounded soldier right now, not interacting or even making eye contact with anyone. We know who's in charge for the time being and I would guess mostly everybody on board is pleased about that state of affairs.

When we reach our destination and the back opens up again, we all make our way down the ramp, moving slowly but with purpose. We're traveling mostly light: M-16s, Claymore anti-personnel mines, and grenades all around.

Except for our commander. He's assigned himself an M-60 machine gun, with two bandoliers of ammunition crisscrossing his torso. Almost like he's expecting a different war from the rest of us.

We march in a careful formation into a village that looks just like a lot of villages we've seen in the past, only it's even smaller than most. Six basic-looking huts, four of which are in some state of burned out. Smoke rises all around us, bits of flame not worth putting out.

And there are bodies. In similarly varied states of charred. I count sixteen, all men, either outside on the ground or straddling doors and windows. Sixteen torsos, that is, with limbs distributed randomly all over the place. Very much an Old West–style shootout aftermath scene, but here in the even older East. We hold our formation and proceed toward the two buildings that remain mostly intact, stepping right around or over bodies. When we come to the first building, Jupp gestures to Bien, who shouts into the place clearly demanding somebody show himself.

We have a whole lot of firepower trained on this one doorway with a canvas drape hanging in it.

Nothing.

Bien shouts some more.

I see my M-16 begin to shake a little as I wait. I am sure, suddenly and for no reason, that there is somebody armed and angry on the other side of that sheet.

We are giving off lots of smells now, our merry band of fighting men. Stronger even than the burning human flesh all around us.

Bien shouts again —

Rat-at-at-at-at-at-at-at-at-at-at-at-at-at!

Without warning, Lt. Jupp unloads on the hut with the M-60, pounding the life out of it, the machine gun sucking in its ammo belt and spitting out bullets at a rate sufficient to kill thirty guys if they were unlucky or stupid enough to be inside. I'm shocked enough to recoil from the impact, and I'm not the only one.

After several seconds and an insane number of rounds, he stops, and we listen while the smoke wafts over us.

"Free-fire, gentlemen!" he says, and despite how supercharged that was, I see his gun muzzle vibrating more than mine. "I think you will find the building is secure."

There is no mistaking that the lieutenant is showing off now, trying to regain some of the top dogness that he lost so much of today.

"McClean, Hunter, Marquette, go in and check that out. The rest of you come with me."

"You shot it all up," Cherry says to him. "Maybe you want to go in and check it out yourself, lieutenant?"

Jupp's small smile slips sideways and right off his face.

There is a *game* going on here. Even I have come to recognize what Lt. Jupp won't be doing under any circumstances — such as going blindly into an enemy hut no matter how many bullets he's pumped into it. And if *I* know it . . .

"Do as you're told, soldiers," Jupp says.

The rest of us follow along, including Cherry, as Jupp swaggers up to the last building. I look back behind me to see the three who were told to go into that hut are very much not going in. They stand there observing what we are up to.

What we are up to is:

Rat-at-at-at-at-at-at-at-at-at-at-at-at-at-at!

The air is again filled with smoke and burn and Jupp's once-again confident voice.

"In you go, Corporal Cherry," he says.

Cherry stands there. "You coming with me?"

Jupp's phony smile tells us all we need to know about what he thinks of this game.

"I gave you an order, Cherry."

"Do you *ever* get your hands dirty, lieutenant?"

I never thought before that *lieutenant* was a dirty word. But the way Cherry says it now, it is filthy.

"Never mind," Squid says, and he starts stomping toward the canvas door.

"Oh no you don't," I shout at my short-timer pal, grabbing him by the backpack and hauling him out of the way. "For crying out loud, I'll do it."

And I do. Before anybody can stop me — not that I can sense anybody thinking of stopping me — I march right up and right through that entrance.

And I scream.

I scream because I fall. It's as if the floor isn't where it's supposed to be. Like I've stepped into a trapdoor that opens onto hell itself.

It is a trapdoor all right, but not quite to hell. Hell wouldn't hurt this bad.

"Ah, ah, ah!" I scream, as the guys surround me. My leg has gone under the floor of the hut, disappearing all the way up to my thigh as the two-piece trapdoor fell away beneath me. All my weight, plus the extra weight of all my gear, has driven me down and right on top of a long metal shaft, like a pencil-thin spike, that has shot right through my boot, my foot, and my boot again. It feels like a lace of fire sizzling up through me.

Cherry and Squid run up and try and pull me out.

"Ahhhhh!" The pain is a hundred times worse when they tug on me. The trapdoors themselves are actually more torture, covered in similar long spikes that close in and clamp on to my leg when I am coming up out of the thing. Like a bear trap of knives. "No, no no, no, stop!"

Squid drops me like I am made of hornets, backs away flapping his hands helplessly. Cherry and Marquette take over, working first to try and wedge the two doors apart.

The pain is making me insane. I try and look at my leg but my vision keeps getting all watery, and my hollering is so intense that it looks like the whole world is quaking instead of just me.

"Lieutenant?" somebody shouts. Then another somebody, then all of them. The guys from the other hut are here now, too, and I see everybody, pretty much, except Jupp.

I finally see Jupp's face, peering over the top of the crowd, looking about a million miles away. Then, I see him yanked right out of the picture as Lt. Bien shoves his way to the front, crouches down over me, and puts both arms down into the trap up to his elbows — just before I pass out, still screaming.

CHAPTER SEVEN

Just a Scratch

There are two letters waiting for me when I come around in the hospital. One is from Ivan, which I save for later like you do with the best part of your supper, and the other is from Morris. Not that Morris is like broccoli or anything, it's just, well, there's only one Ivan.

Hey Rudi Man,

I guess this is overdue, huh? I had two letters from you before I even got one back to you. Sorry about that but, jeez, who'd have ever thought you would turn out to be the big writer of the group, right? Anyway, the good part is, I got my wish and I'm a radioman now, so I'm going to be calling you once I get the hang of tracking you guys down. One of the perks of my job, you see, is being able to make phone calls just like we were back home and I needed to ask you a math question or something. (That's a joke, Rudi, pay attention.)

The war has been ok for me so far. As much as wars can be ok. I'm not dead, which is a plus. At least I don't think I am. When I was on the USS <u>Boston</u>, we got hit — by our own guys! And I think I survived that, although I may be dead and just don't recognize dead yet.

I am in the Brown Water Navy now, pal. Which might very well be what death looks and feels and smells like. We are in the thick of things all the time, shooting it out with the VC all up and down the Mekong. I am on a Zippo. You know, like the cigarette lighters? We've got napalm flamethrowers mounted on this thing. It's crazy what all different kinds of killing gear we have on this one boat. And for defense? It's mostly caging and sandbags. We get shot at all the time.

I had a pal, pal. He was on both the <u>Boston</u> and the Zippo with me. Not a pal like you guys, nobody will ever be that. But a pal still. He got killed. My God, Rudi, when a pal gets killed . . .

We don't ever want that to happen. That's the big thing. Never.

But enough about me, let's talk about me.

Just kidding. How about you? I have to say there was quite a leap between the first letter you sent me and the second. Really, really great that you fit so well in the Marines. I was happy — and shocked — to hear how well that was going. Because, to be honest . . . ah, well you know. We all secretly peed ourselves, on your behalf, when you got drafted. It's good that you're so good at following orders. It's good that you found an organization that can appreciate your particular talents.

That second letter, Rudi man, I have to say was an eye opener. Confirmed killer now. Wow. I mean it. Wow. Me, I don't know. I mean, sure, I shoot, they insist I do more than sit on the phone all day since that's not likely to advance the cause much, so I do shoot at people on a pretty regular basis. But I don't know for sure if I ever hit anybody or not. And to be honest with you, I don't want to know. I would like to return home as much like I was before as possible. Who'd have ever thought, huh man? That this young, we would be handling this kind of firepower? That we would be controlling people's whole lives with our decisions every day?

But you. You KNOW, don't you? There is no maybe in your close-combat world. You have killed, Rudi. I just got a chill when I wrote that down, you know that kind of thing that zings up your spine and back down again?

There is certain stuff a guy just has to do. I am really impressed that you have found yourself able to do whatever it takes. So do whatever it takes to get yourself home in one piece. We want you home.

You. We want you home. Our old Rudi. Remember, doofus, you don't have to like it. Just because you have to do it doesn't mean you have to like it.

I will try to get a call through to you soon. Meanwhile, watch yourself and keep safe.

Your pal,
Morris

Here's the thing you have to love about Morris. He's a really smart guy, but he doesn't act like it. Beck, for example, is a great guy. But he's a really smart guy who acts like a really smart guy. That's not as good.

Here's what you don't have to love about Morris, or at least I don't. He's not in charge of me. He's not my mother or my teacher or my priest or my commanding officer. I don't have to do what he says to do because I don't have to want what he wants. I'm no kid anymore, which maybe he can't understand because he can't see me.

And maybe he wants to see the same old Rudi come home, and maybe that's nice of him. But I don't want to bring that idiot home. I don't ever want to see him again, to tell you the truth, and that's up to me no matter what Morris says.

I was smart to save my Ivan letter for dessert. Because while all three of my best buddies are still my best buddies, the guy who is most likely to understand what I'm doing and where I'm going is always going to be Ivan. He's not going to come up all brainy like Beck would or all parental like Morris. He's just built different.

Hi,

YOU GOTTA STOP IT, RUDI.

OK, THAT MAYBE WASN'T THE BEST WAY TO START THIS BUT YOU KNOW I AIN'T MUCH OF A WRITER AND YOU AIN'T MUCH OF A READER SO IT'S BEST FOR EVERYBODY IF I JUST GET RIGHT IN AND RIGHT OUT HERE.

YOU GOTTA STOP SAYING YOU ARE DOING EVERYTHING FOR ME. IT IS GREAT OF YOU TO SAY SO, BUT I DON'T WANT THAT, MAN, YOU UNDERSTAND? YOU GOTTA DO STUFF FOR YOURSELF, BECOME THE SOLDIER YOU WANT TO BE FOR YOURSELF. IF I HAVE HELPED YOU IN ANY WAY TO BECOME MORE OF A MAN AND BE LESS AFRAID AND BE MAYBE A LITTLE TOUGHER (WELL, LET'S HOPE A LOT TOUGHER) THAN YOU WERE BEFORE YOU SHIPPED OUT, THEN THAT IS ENOUGH FOR ME TO KNOW. IF YOU SERVE YOUR COUNTRY AND SERVE YOUR UNIT AND SERVE YOUR-SELF IN AN HONORABLE AND SUCCESSFUL MANNER THEN THAT IS ALL THAT ANYBODY CAN ASK. DO YOUR JOB THE BEST YOU CAN AND GROW UP AND THEN GET HOME AGAIN. I AM PROUD OF YOU. I WAS PROUD OF YOU WHEN YOU GOT ON THE BOAT OUT OF OAKLAND (REALLY,

IT WAS ONLY THEN THAT I COMPLETELY BELIEVED) INSTEAD OF THE BUS TO CANADA. FROM THIS POINT ON YOU DON'T NEED TO IMPRESS ME ANY FURTHER. GOT IT?

THINGS ARE GOING OK HERE. I'M A SNIPER, WHICH IS GOOD.

SO, I MEAN IT, IF YOU GET YOURSELF ALL KILLED OR INJURED I WILL SLAP YOU SILLY YA LITTLE JERK.

BEST WISHES,
IVAN
P.S. I MEAN IT.

I am laughing out loud now because of course he doesn't mean it, which is making my leg hurt even more. Which makes me laugh even more because this injury would make Ivan slap me silly — both because of all what he just said, and because slapping me silly was just always something he liked to do. I miss it. It's time for my medication.

The hospital at the base at Chu Lai is probably about as fancy as you could expect for being right smack in the middle of everything. It's kind of like a small airplane hangar with a row of big baby cribs lined up along each side, and long fluorescent strip lights hanging over each one. The nurse who has been taking care of me mostly is named Carolyn and she is very tall and slim with black moppy hair, and while she is a little bit intimidating from my angle she is kind enough to be much smaller than she is.

"Here ya go, dingbat," she says, bringing me my little cup of pain pills and another cup of water. I swallow both quickly while she leans on the rails of my baby crib. I find the rails embarrassing, but do enjoy the leaning. She's called me dingbat from the minute I got here even though she couldn't even have known yet.

"When I get out of here would you like to go out with me sometime?" I ask, and I get a rush from just the asking. I can't even believe I'm doing it. Because that's just not like me at all, to even be able to talk to a tall girl. Somehow, now it's easy.

"You know, I never get asked that," she says.

"Really? Wow. That's great because I would imagine with all the —"

"See now, sweetie, I was just joking with you there. Know what I mean? There are like fifty million servicemen for every nurse, and by the time I see them they are not only wounded and needy and looking for their mommy, but they are also medicated. So, sweet as you are . . . I am *awfully* more popular than I need to be already. But on the bright side, you do have visitors."

"Cabbage!" the guys yelp before Carolyn shushes them down. It's Hunter and Squid and Marquette. Carolyn moves on to the next crib, and they all start giving me the eyes like I'm Mr. Lucky or something. Then all three produce what look like sharpened chopsticks and start poking me with them, hard.

"Ow, I get it, ow, I get it," I say, twisting as far away from them as my cage bed will allow me to. "I could go a long time without getting stabbed with sticks again, I can tell you that."

"Oh," Hunter says, "about that. We have decided to change your nickname to Pincushion. How's that, Cabbage?"

"No," I say. "As a matter of fact, you might want to consider calling me Rudi."

"Rudi?" Marquette says. "That's a stupid name. Why would we want to call you that?"

"Yeah," I say. "I suppose. What are you doing here, anyway? I thought I was GI Joke to you?"

"You are GI Joke. But you're *our* joke. And you got guts, Cabbage, I have to give you that. You ain't satisfied to sit back and let somebody else do the dirty work, that's for sure. So, even if you are a dummy, I can appreciate that."

"Thanks," I say. "It's nice to be appreciated."

"You are," Squid says, and he hands me a coloring book and a box of crayons. It has sixty-four colors in it, which is a lot.

I look up at him to try and tell if this is a joke gift, but he has such a giant stupid grin on his face I don't suppose it matters much either way.

And I don't even feel like I need to embarrass myself further by telling them how much I still like coloring books when I'm bored. Especially Superman coloring books like this one.

"Thanks, guys," I say.

"So," Hunter asks, "how's the leg? I gotta tell you, man, it was pretty disgusting to look at at first."

"At first?" I say. "How 'bout this?" I whip back the covers to show off my foot and leg, which are swollen to only about twice normal size now.

"*Ahhh.*" All three brave warriors shrink away from the bed, recoiling as if I've released a deep-sea monster from under the sheet. Which is not far off.

The color and texture of the leg is like a relief map of the central highlands, all swirly green and purple bruising, punctuated by splats of stitching and ooze leaking out yellow here and there onto the sheet.

"Oh, put it away, put it away," Marquette says, laughing and gagging at the same time.

When I cover up again they return to my bedside.

"The shots they give me to fight infection are the worst part," I say. "Because of the dung they put on the spike tips, man, they have to give me regular injections they shoot right into the wounds. Kinda hurts, kinda a whole lot."

"Yeoo," Squid says.

"Yeoo is right. Man, I am itching to get back out there. How's it all going, anyway?"

"Eh," Hunter says, "it's kind of gone back to the way it was before. A lot of pointless patrols, a little bit of shooting into the trees, but nothing like all the fun we had when you were around."

"What about the corporals? The lieutenant?"

"Please," Marquette says, disgusted.

"Things are kind of tense, kind of worse than before," Hunter says. "Nobody talks to nobody else. Nobody seems to want to do anything but watch the clock tick off the days, and just get out."

"I got two and a half weeks, Cabbage," Squid says brightly.

"I know it," I say, matching his tone but not quite his enthusiasm. I can't shake the feeling that he was right before — a lot could happen in two and a half weeks.

"And Sunshine, man," Hunter says, "he's darker

than he ever was and getting worse all the time. He needs to do a lot more shooting than he's doing now. Needs an outlet to blow off some very scary steam."

"Yeah," Marquette says, looking partly cloudy himself at the moment. "I'll tell you what, if somebody —"

"Hey, dingbat," Carolyn says, sweeping back in with more company, "you win our Private Popular prize today."

Walking right up to me behind her is Lt. Jupp.

Marquette doesn't even say anything as he turns and walks out.

"Okay," Squid says, leaving next. "Get better, man, and get back to us. I would hate to go home without fighting alongside you one more time, man, and that's the truth."

I don't know if I have heard a nicer compliment since I've been here. Or before that, either.

"See, ya, Cabbage," Hunter says, and swoops off.

"Well, I guess that's just the loneliness of command," Jupp says, laughing without laughing. "If I come around every day, maybe the hospital will empty out completely and we'll be at twice the strength in battle."

"Ah, lieutenant, they were just leaving anyway," I say. "You'd be surprised how quick a talk between grunts can get stupid boring."

"Maybe I would," he says, "maybe I wouldn't."

"And besides," I say, "I had a lot of serious paperwork to get to." I hold up my Superman coloring book.

He smiles, in a kind of sad way I have not seen before. I didn't want that.

"How are you, Cabbage?" he says softly. I don't want that, either. I want him to shout unnecessarily like he always does, because this other thing is making me uneasy. But I know he can't shout because it's a hospital.

"I'm good, sir. Just getting through these last stages of healing so they'll give me the all-clear to come back and fight for you."

He shakes his head. "You are something, private. A lot of men would want no part of coming back after what happened. You know . . . if you wanted to . . . this is enough of an injury to send you back to . . . where are you from again?"

"Boston. And I don't want to go there. I am a Marine, sir, and this is where I should be. Well, not here, exactly. I don't like sleeping in a bed with side rails for one thing. But here in Vietnam, or wherever the fighting takes me, is where I belong."

There are a number of little things going on here that would look kind of nice to somebody just walking in but that I am finding not all that great. He's being really nice, the lieutenant, in an odd way that seems to have him looking over his shoulder as if somebody might catch him at it. And a couple of times already he has patted me on the leg — the good one, not the one with the holes in it — while he's talking to me.

"You're a good kid, Rudi," he says. "And you are a good soldier. Best in this outfit, that's for sure. Better than me, I can tell you that."

"Oh, jeez, lieutenant . . ."

"No, no, it's the truth. The thing is, with this war being what it is, with this force being what it is, it can be dispiriting. The Marines, frankly, have had to drop their standards lower and lower as this thing has dragged on, to the point where you don't want to trust anybody with anything. I was different when I first joined up, different when I first came to Vietnam. This is my second tour, did you know that?"

"No, sir, I didn't. I heard some guys actually get out of here and then come back again of their own free will, but I don't expect I run into them too often."

"Ha. Well, you're looking at one right here. But I'll tell you, kid, and this is important so listen close. I had just about bottomed out these past months, for all the good reasons. I've been just hanging on 'til I could be done with this whole insane thing and get back to the real world. In the meantime, I became a bad leader and a lousy fighting man. But you know what? Something about you, Rudi, has made me think I could still do something while I'm here. A man has to have something to drive him on, and I've decided you're gonna be that something, or at least a big part of that something, during the remainder of my tour. I am going to make something of all this."

"All this, sir?"

"All this. This situation. I am going to make something of it. I am going to get back to the fighting man I was. I am going to give it all I have. And before I go, I am going to give *you* all I have, to help you to become the best fighting man possible. Because I think you have a future in this, Marine. And because in all the time I've been here, you have given more of yourself to it than anyone I've seen."

I can't do anything but stare at him. I can't believe what I have heard, and I am a little bit choked up about it. It is beyond the point of weirdness to feel optimistic about war, but he has kind of given me that.

He salutes me.

I salute back.

Then he offers me a firm handshake.

"Thank you," he says, then backs away. "See you back on the line soon, soldier."

"Yes, sir," I say, still a little thrown. I watch him

walk away, all the way down between the lines of big baby beds.

"So how was that, dingbat?" Carolyn says, passing by and tweaking my big toe on her way to somebody else.

"It was good," I say, my voice a little floaty as I dig into my box of sixty-four and open up my Superman book.

CHAPTER EIGHT

Boomtown

I wanted to get back as soon as I could, and I wanted maybe to get back too soon.

Squid is walking with me as I make my way out of the hospital and across the big compound that is the Chu Lai base. I could have taken a ride to my quarters, but I am feeling so good, so ready, and so lacking in fitness I figure a good hike is the best thing. Squid, being Squid, decided to come meet me and escort me home.

Halfway there I am wondering how good an idea this really is.

"That looks like a lot more of a limp than it was a few minutes ago," he says, looking down at my leg for answers.

"That's 'cause it hurts a lot more than it did a few minutes ago."

"You sure you're all right?" he asks.

"Well, yes and no. I'm all right, meaning I should be out of the hospital. I'm not all right, meaning my leg is not as great as it was before the alligator bit it. It's just gotta heal, man, and this is nothing but another stage in that process."

Or possibly I pushed to get out of the hospital just a little bit too early. Anyway, there's no going back, so we go forward.

By the time we reach the hooch I am as exhausted as I would normally be after a ten-mile hike. There is nobody around, which makes it a perfect time to throw myself down for some rest.

"What do you think about getting something to eat?" Squid asks.

"I'm good, man. They gave me a sandwich before shoving me on my way."

"Okay then. You want me to stick around? 'Cause if not I think I'll try and get some chow since lunch is almost over."

"Go, man, go," I say. "Thanks for the escort. I'll see you later."

"Sure thing," he says, and trots off to the mess.

It's funny, but my return here to the hooch, after not even that much time, feels important. Meaningful. Maybe it was the injury. The mission, the killings, becoming a real soldier and a real man. Maybe it was being separated from my squad for the first time, after being separated from my original squad of Ivan, Morris, and Beck. Maybe it was all of those things and more. But I feel like I am needed here, with these men, and I feel like I need them, too.

I am thinking all this as I drift off, lying on my back, my arm over my eyes, smiling —

Booo-booooooooom!

The explosion doesn't knock me out of bed, but my reaction to it sure does. That blast was *close*, as in right-around-the-corner close, and I hit the floor and remain there on all fours like a dozy dog for several seconds. Then there is commotion and chaos outside, and I jump up and grab my helmet and rifle and run toward the action along with everybody else.

My leg is killing me when I get to the scene, but my leg killing me is nothing, man.

Nothing.

It's Lt. Jupp's quarters. Or it used to be. Now it is a smoldering hole in the ground.

It's called *fragging*.

It has been around in different forms for probably as long as there have been armies. It is what happens when you put men in battle and under pressure, and you put some men in charge and tell other men they have to do whatever they are told. And all those men are armed and trained and highly dangerous. And some of those men disagree seriously with their superiors and some of those men hate their superiors and all of them have the opportunity to get away with something. Something like murder.

In Vietnam, it got to be called *fragging* because it is often accomplished by throwing a fragmentation grenade into somebody's space. That's what Lt. Jupp got.

Fragmented.

In a way, I feel like I got that, too.

But he's the one who's now in a zillion unpopular pieces, rather than just the one he was in before. He wasn't a bad guy. He wasn't. He wasn't he wasn't. He wasn't a coward or a bully or a monster or a traitor or a dope or a racist or a communist or a clown or an oaf or an ogre or a tool or a waster or a whiner or a diner or a diddler or a fiddler or any of the fifty hundred thousand million other names I've heard here, hung on guys who other guys think should be dead. He wasn't.

He was loud. And he was worn out. And he was coming back.

He was on the right side. He was on our side.

He was on my side.

"Do you realize," asks the very tall and very blond and very slouched man in the chair on the other side of the makeshift desk that is really more of a card table, "how many members of the NIS, among the several hundred thousand service personnel and several million indigenous individuals, are presently in the country of South Vietnam?"

He is referring to the Naval Investigative Service, which is responsible for looking into possible crimes involving United States Navy and Marine Corps personnel. He is squeezing his great bony temples with his long bony fingers as he asks me this.

"I would have no idea what the answer to that question is, sir."

He squeezes his temples some more. Sweat drains from them, like he is squeezing fresh lemonade from a lemon. I am thirsty.

"Were you ever on a football team, son? Perhaps in high school or with a Pop Warner league?"

"No, sir." I would have thought he could have worked that out for himself already. If the guy knows what a jock looks like he knows it doesn't look like me. But he does seem awfully tired.

"Know anybody else who was on a team?"

"Ivan," I say. "Ivan was great. He played both ways. All-conference as both a linebacker and fullback."

"Swell," he says. "Good for Ivan. Well, if you look back at that team, those on the offense plus those on defense, that is about how many members, total, of the NIS are here in-country."

Wow, I'm thinking.

"Wow, sir."

" 'Wow.' Yes. So, son, we need to be lean and hungry with our investigations. Right? You understand that, right?"

"Right."

"So, did you kill Lt. Jupp?"

It makes me want to puke to even hear that question.

"No, sir."

"You are aware that he was killed within the hour after you got back to your quarters?"

"Yes, sir."

"Within the hour after your return from a hospital stay for a deeply serious and deeply unpleasant injury that happened while you were doing the business assigned to you in the field under Lt. Jupp."

"Yes, sir, I am aware of all that."

"And you were not with any of the other men at the time of the incident, is that correct, private?"

"Correct."

"So, you know why I would be asking you such a question."

"Yes, sir."

"So then, I will ask you again. Did you kill Lt. Jupp?"

It doesn't get any less sickening to be asked a second time. I don't figure it will get any less sickening if he asks me five million times. It will probably just get worse.

"No, sir, I did not."

He continues, for a minute, to squeeze lemonade from his head. Then he looks up and right at me.

"I know that, sweetheart," he says. "Now, can you tell me who did?"

Cripes. Where to even begin with this? Well, let's begin with how much I don't want to be here. Then move on to how much I don't want to be here.

Lt. Jupp is dead.

Somebody here probably killed him.

My brain is not big enough for this. Who would do this kind of thing? There are plenty of guys around here who seemed at one time or another angry enough at the lieutenant to say or do or *not* do something stupid, but to kill him? I can't fit that into my head. I just can't believe there is any single guy here who would be capable of that.

We kill, sure. But we're not *killers*. That's a whole 'nother thing, isn't it? Isn't it?

"I have no idea, sir. That's the truth."

"Gillespie could do something like that, couldn't he, private."

I would never say anyone was capable of doing that.

If I ever would say such a thing, though, I might say it about Gillespie.

"No, sir," I say, "I could not imagine that."

"Lt. Jupp was not a popular man, was he, private."

"I couldn't say, sir."

"Actually, you *could* say, son. And you had better say, or risk a charge of obstructing the investigation of a very tired and overworked man who has to cover one-twenty-fourth of a country of sixty-five thousand square miles in which fraggings are currently occurring at the rate of about one per week. Now . . . from what I can gather so far you were on a list of Lt. Jupp's favorite subordinates, a list that extended to approximately one. You. The other men mostly hated him and vice versa."

"Squid doesn't hate anybody, sir."

"You know, fair enough. Spoke to that Squid fellow and I believe that to be accurate. Am I to gather from this that you are now cooperating by process of elimination and that any of your other squad mates could have been responsible?"

Every time I say something I feel like I'm in deeper. Every time I say nothing I feel likewise.

"I don't think Hunter could have done it, either."

"Now we're getting somewhere," he says.

And I can't take it anymore.

"No, sir, we aren't getting somewhere. Because I don't believe any of the guys could have done this. Maybe it was just an accident. They do happen, don't they? There's a lot of dangerous stuff around here. . . ."

Up 'til now, he's been taking notes. Now, he stops writing. Puts his pen in his pocket, closes his notebook.

"I'll give you credit, son," he says, standing from the card table. "It took you longer to get to that than every other one of 'em. Truth is, unless somebody confesses or rats out somebody else, there is practically nothing we can do these days. This place is all but lawless now. I wish you luck, kid, I really do. Because once it gets to this point . . . well, good luck, is all. And watch your back."

He shakes my hand and walks to the door.

I sit, alone again, not knowing what to do with myself next.

The new lieutenant wants to see me. It's not that I'm special, though — he's having sit-downs with everybody. One by one the guys go to see him in his hooch, and one by one they come back calling the next guy. There is little exchange of information during the changeover, just as there is little communication at all since Jupp's killing. It isn't that nobody trusts anybody.

It's that everybody doesn't trust somebody. And we are not even sure who that somebody is.

I have to change that statement. I sort of don't trust anybody.

I don't expect to get shot or blown up by one of our own guys. No, a person has to be important in some way for that to happen, and I am basic-level grunt all the way. What worries me is that, when it comes down to it, I'm beginning to think that the guys here are of a mind to look out for themselves instead of each other. That's what I'm feeling now, and for a fighting force that's about as poisonous as it can get.

"Trust me," McClean says as he steps into the hooch and points that I'm up next, "this guy's gonna be an even bigger pain than Jupp."

I get off my bunk and walk past him on the way to the door.

"Know who I trusted?" I say. "I trusted Lieutenant Jupp."

I did. Despite it all, I did.

All those kissy-kissy noises follow me out the door and I don't know who's doing it and I don't even care to look.

Lieutenant Silva's hooch is like an indoor cloud. It's as if somebody has let off a white phosphorus flare in there, except maybe more like a blue-gray phosphorus flare. He is lighting one cigarette off of another one when I enter, and he's sitting on one folding canvas chair, with his feet propped up on a second and his overflowing ashtray on a third. Looks like a fire hazard.

I remain standing.

"No beating around any bushes with me, kid, okay?"

"Okay," I say.

"I like you," he says.

"Thank you, sir. I didn't even realize you knew me."

"I know you by record and reputation, private. Mind if I call you Rudi?"

"Most guys around here call me Cabbage, lieutenant."

"Uh-huh. Mind if I call you Rudi?"

"I don't mind at all, sir."

"Good. Now here is the way I figure we're gonna understand each other. I will give out orders and assignments. And you will follow those orders and assignments. I will hold up my end of the bargain by not making any unreasonable demands of the soldiers under me as far as I can help it, and I will fight shoulder to shoulder with those soldiers like the partners in crime that we actually are. In exchange for this respect I offer you, you will agree not to kill me or to maim me, nor to attempt to kill or maim me. How's that sound to you? Because it sounds eminently fair and rea-sonable to me."

Lt. Silva has sucked down that cigarette in about the time it would take most people to suck down a Dixie cup of soda. He lights another one.

"Sounds fair and reasonable, lieutenant."

"Good," he says. "Good. Rudi, my man, here is what I understand about you. You are the prototype of a loyal and dedicated Marine. Would you say that is fair?"

"I like to think it is." I'd also like to think I knew what a prototype is, but I'll settle for the other good words I recognize in there.

"Good. Fair is good. I am a fair man, and fairness is never far from my thoughts. I am guessing you feel like-wise. Fair enough?"

I did not expect to smile in this meeting at all. I am pleasantly surprised.

"Fair enough," I say.

"And while you have the aforementioned invaluable qualities and probably a whole lot more, I think it is equally fair to state that you are not the brightest booby in the trap. *Is* that true, and *does* that hurt your feel-ings, Rudi?"

"It certainly is, and it certainly does not, sir," I say, and it's probably extra stupid now to be grinning like I am, but so what since I won't be fooling anybody here about my brightness or lack thereof, anyway.

He is smiling now, too, and smoking and nodding. "We're going to be able to work together just fine, son. You will learn that you get a lot of slack from me, a lot of free-run if you just give me honesty and effort. You will be on a long leash. Free-fire means free-fire now. The brass want body counts. They do not want American body counts. Our job is to make those two wishes come true."

This is making me smile too hard.

"I see you are smiling. That's a good thing. But in light of this squad's history I don't encourage you to get too giddy there, Rudi. It's a fact of life that the people you think you know, you do not know. The people you think you could never know, you may well know them all too well. What you think is most likely always wrong. Do you see a lesson in there somewhere, private?"

I was really hoping I had left lessons back in high school, which was about fifty years ago now. But I believe I know what he's getting at.

"Don't think, sir?"

"Perfect. You are the perfect soldier, son."

Wow. Is that the key? I wish I knew that before. I would have enlisted when I was nine. I'd have General Westmoreland's job by now.

"Unless you have any questions, you can go now, Rudi. But I want you to know that you can come and ask me anything at any time. Communication is key. Understood?"

"Understood," I say.

"How's the leg, by the way?"

"Good," I say. "Perfect. Ready to go out and do some stomping." Then, I turn to go.

"And hey," he calls just as I get through the doorway.

"Yes?"

"You are the finest Marine in the whole outfit. That's the word, and I believe the word."

I don't say anything to Silva, because what are you supposed to say to that? I do say something to myself, though, inside. I say: *How much you want to bet he said that same thing to each guy, one by one by one by whoever?* Okay, maybe not *every* one, but still.

As I make my way back to our quarters, I have to shake my head in disbelief at how Cpl. McClean could come away from a conversation with that man thinking that we were going to have difficulties ahead. Makes me realize just how far away I feel from grasping this situation right now.

I hear, as I near the hooch, a lot of commotion. It is angry commotion, and the kind you quick-up your step to see.

I rush around to the side of our hooch, the narrow strip of dirt that runs between it and the corrugated metal wall of the storage building behind us. There's a fight going on. It's between Marquette and Gillespie, and it is furious. I've never seen so many punches thrown in such a short span of time in my life, and I grew up watching ice hockey. Both guys are shirtless, so they can't get a grip on each other. They are slippery with sweat and blood, so there's not much to do but punch.

And they are hammering, while all the other guys stand around them, watching and murmuring low enough to not attract a whole big lot of attention. It's also like hockey in that the authorities will let a lot of this go on without intervening, to let the boys get it out, as long as they're not too public about it. The thinking is they will get it out, and that will be that.

They are getting it out all right. Especially Gillespie. He is taking some hits, but he is dishing out probably two-for-one in the punching, and it seems like every shot he gets through gets there with a fire and precision and hate that is already making him the winner though he has not finished yet with the punishment.

Marquette's forehead is bleeding from a massive gash over his left eye, and his mouth is so pulpy it looks like somebody is force-feeding him overripe tomatoes.

Sunshine has a shiner for a left eye, but not much else for damage. As Marquette loses steam and drops his hands some, Gillespie finds new inspiration and throws his whole self behind a vicious left hand that knows just exactly what its mission is.

I am about five feet away, and I can hear the crisp snap as Marquette's nose is broken.

It is, truly, stomach churning, in a way that catches me completely by surprise. My stomach is doing flips and my knees are shaky, seeing one of our own guys destroying another, watching the blood puddle up in the sand between them. The corporals are both loving it, but Hunter looks shocked into numbness.

Squid, though, is a picture of horror. His right hand is covering his mouth, and his eyes are all soupy with near-tears.

The punching stops. With Gillespie, it is voluntary, but for Marquette's part there is no choice involved. There is a brief pause, then Sunshine takes two steps straight back, just in time for Marquette to fall almost right onto the winner's toes.

You know what that was? That was violence. Real violence. More than the other war stuff.

"Yours'll come, Gillespie," Marquette says from face-down in the mud. He sounds like he's talking through Jell-O and grit and lumpy mashed potatoes.

Gillespie leans down over him, says in a rasp, "Call me Sunshine."

He turns, picks up his shirt, and leaves without another word, headed, I would guess, for the showers. The corporals huddle-walk in the opposite direction, talking all low and excited. Hunter inches over and crouches down near Marquette as he tries to get up. Marquette makes it to his hands and knees, then just stays there for several seconds until Hunter helps him the rest of the way to his feet. They make their way around to the door of the hooch, where Hunter will for sure be the good man nurse until he can talk Marquette into visiting the good gal nurse.

Squid stands there, like he's petrified. Standing, staring at the stupid bloody mud on the ground. Flies are on it already, which seems both repulsive and perfect to me.

I step over to Squid, push his hand down from his mouth. "Don't be a baby," I say. "Or, at least, don't let anybody see you being a baby."

He keeps staring, shaking his head a little. So I grab him by the front tail of his shirt, and I tow him, tugging him along behind me all the way back to Lt. Silva's hooch. I knock on the door frame. We enter the fog.

"You said I could ask you anything, sir?"

"You can always ask."

"Could you send Squid home, sir? He has less than two weeks left as it is. He's already done enough and seen enough, and the truth is that I won't be letting him do anything dangerous or useful or anything that will put him within spitting distance of sniffing distance of harm's way, so he's no more use to us and could even be a hindrance, what with me having to look out for him and all. And his dad's not doing so good and he really needs to get back and see him. And . . . no beating around any bushes, sir?"

"Absolutely none, private."

"This is frankly not a situation that can benefit the boy at all now."

Silva lights a cigarette off a cigarette, blows smoke straight up into the air as if there is a free space up there anywhere.

"And if I say you will have to put in twice the effort over the coming weeks to make up for Squid's lost man-power?"

"I say, fair enough," I say.

Squid says nothing. Doesn't appear quite capable at the moment.

"Rudi, do you think young Squid here might do something drastic if he can't get away from this place

ASAP?" He has a comically earnest look on his face as he asks this.

"I wouldn't care to speculate on such a thing, lieutenant," I say. "At this point, I wouldn't speculate on anything or anyone in Vietnam."

CHAPTER NINE

Rudi 2-D

I may well go down as the soldier who went through the greatest number of nicknames during his tour of Vietnam.

There is no more play left in this squad, and that is beyond dispute. Nicknames don't come with the same bounce they did before. Even when we call Gillespie Sunshine to his face now, it's not because it's a funny joke — which it is — but more because we're almost afraid not to.

Mine is something wildly different now, and it comes, in fact, from Sunshine.

We are out on patrol, which we do nearly every morning now with Lt. Silva. He refuses to let us hang day after day at the base, getting somehow both bored and tense, like we did before. He does his research, his homework, and somehow manages to get us assignments that more or less straddle the line between dangerous and pointless. Most of the time we visit villages that intelligence suggests are swinging in the breeze between friendly and hostile. To do this day after day is a guarantee that you don't lose your edge, because dropping your guard is well known to be the express route to dead.

I have never yet worked out a reliable method for deciding which of the local people are innocently going about the business of living and which are hoping to skin me like a rabbit supper. Really, I have seen families floating by on a river in a sampan and they couldn't look any more innocent if they had Winnie the Pooh and Tigger and Christopher Robin on board serving cupcakes. Then, twenty meters downstream, those same people unload a handful of grenades at an American River Monitor like the boat my pal Morris is on and half the crew are dead. Of course, the family winds up dead, too, but that hardly makes it all worthwhile, does it?

It makes you tense, is what it does. It makes you possibly not all the way sane. You have to find a way to deal with it. Every single guy here has to find a way.

I guess I found a way without even knowing it.

"Holy *moly*," Cpl. McClean says when he kicks at what looks like a suitcase handle sticking out of the dirt. It is just outside a hut, a hut like a hundred other huts we've seen, in a tiny abandoned village we have just combed for personnel and weapons. He reaches down, brushes away some leaf cover, and we find the handle attached to a door.

Which, we realize, is attached to a tunnel.

"Oh boy, oh boy," Lt. Silva says. "I have been looking for these things forever. There are said to be *thousands* of miles of these tunnels, men. Mostly up in the central highlands, but all over the rest of the country as well, and yet my luck's so rotten I never ever come across them."

"Until now," Hunter says.

"Until now," Silva says excitedly.

"So what do you suppose is in there?" Cherry asks.

"Anything and everything," Silva says. "The more extensive ones I've heard about are built over two or even three levels. They got kitchens down there, and bathrooms, workshops for building stuff, and room after room for storing weapons and ammunition. Some of these things are so sophisticated they really contain whole miniature cities, and can serve as delivery depots for stuff arriving here all the way from the Ho Chi Minh Trail in Cambodia."

"And some of them are just little ol' burrows under little ol' nothin' villages," Marquette says flatly.

"And some of them are that," Silva says.

McClean pulls up the lid to reveal a wood-framed hole about eighteen inches by eighteen inches. And very, very dark.

"Pretty inviting," says Sunshine.

"Indeed," says Silva.

Now, here's how it is with me, how it's been since basically the explosion, the shift in command, the fight, the whole change of scene here: I don't talk much. I've decided it's a soldier's job to take orders, to listen about twenty times as much as he talks. And so I will exchange information, I will communicate in a helpful and professional manner, but beyond that . . . the idea of just talking to the other guys, without a specific reason, never appeals to me much. I'd just as soon keep to myself. I'm not rude or impolite, not mean or snarly. I would say even that in my way I might be the best mannered man in this outfit. Like a silent and gentle monk, most of the time.

My nickname for the past two weeks has been Private Monk.

Hunter, I would consider a friend. I talk to him here and there without a compelling reason to. I would bet just about anything that Hunter hasn't killed anybody he wasn't supposed to. As for all the rest up and down that line?

I couldn't tell you a thing for sure. But I would imagine that whatever they have done, each one of them would tell you they believed they did the right thing, for the right reason. And they'd believe it, no doubt about it.

"This has to be investigated," Lt. Silva says about the tunnel.

A few things are obvious right out of the chute. Sunshine, Marquette, and Silva are definitely too big for the job, and probably McClean as well. That leaves me, Cherry, and Hunter, and Cpl. Cherry wouldn't go into a tunnel if you filled it with water and set him on fire. Possibly no corporal in the entire corps would, from what I've been able to gather.

Here's another thing I'm aware of, as I look at Hunter go a bit whiter at the prospect of the tunnel: It is time for me to speak.

"Lt. Silva, as I understand it a man cannot be sent down into one of them tunnels unless he volunteers to do so."

Silva smiles. "You understand correctly, private."

"I'm going down that tunnel, sir. Like yourself, I've been hearing about these tunnels for a long time without encountering one. And like you, I am very excited at the discovery. But unlike you, lieutenant, I am built for the job."

Now Hunter smiles, though he tries not to.

"Are you calling me fat, private?" Lt. Silva says.

For a second I panic, then I calm as I see Silva grinning like a skeleton head with a cigarette clenched between his teeth. There isn't any fat on him. He's just big.

"I do believe that's more words than Private Monk has spoken all month," Sunshine says.

"Come on, come on," I say, and find a weird kind of franticness come over me, an itch to get down that tunnel. "Let's get me kitted out for this job, men," I say.

"Right," Silva says. "We need a light, a pistol, a knife . . ."

I get more excited with every item he lists. I'm getting some kind of mania coming over me, rushing from the ground up. Heart's pounding, head's spinning, but there's nothing bad about what's happening to me because I'm seeing right now with a clarity I haven't had for a long time, if ever.

I am supposed to be doing this, right now. I was meant for this. I feel as correct about going under the ground in the next few minutes as if I was some kind of giant diamond-head drill bit gonna bore all the way to the center of the earth.

And I think it shows.

"Look at this boy, wouldja?" Sunshine says. "Who is this guy? This is a whole other-dimension Rudi we are seeing here. Second-dimension Rudi. Rudi 2-D, that's who we have here."

I like it as soon as I hear it.

I like it more than all my other names combined.

Rudi 2-D. That's who's going down into this tunnel. The original Rudi never could have done this in a million years. The original test-failing, fight-losing, pants-wetting, dead-weight loser Rudi could never have done this, ever, ever. In any life. Ever.

And what's more. What's more? Most other people couldn't do this, either. Not on their best, bravest day.

"Thanks, man," Hunter says as he secures the flashlight to my chest with some white medical tape. When I am in there crawling, this will act like the headlight on an underground train.

"No problem, man," I say. "Happy to do it."

"I didn't even know that thing about needing volunteers for this. That true?"

"True, but I would've done it anyway."

"Yeah, well, I wouldn't have. Even if they ordered me. I'd have let them court martial me first."

"Ah," I say, shoving him away, "no, you wouldn't."

He just grins, and I figure, yeah, he probably would have.

Sunshine has detached his bayonet and shoved it into my hand. He is grinning and shaking his head at the same time. "Go get 'em," he says.

Lt. Silva detaches his own sidearm from his hip, checks the clip, then slaps it back into place before handing it over. "Some guys get all the fun," he says.

I nod at him. Silva would do this, and so would Sunshine. That's it.

I am sitting on the edge of the hole, about to be lowered down, when a thought flashes in my head, because I am still — at least for another second, until I drop down under the ground of this country on the opposite side of life from my life — I am still one little small part the sad Rudy-Judy from Boston:

Morris would never do this.

Beck would never do this.

Arthur and Teddy and every other fathead who threw my books and pencils and tuna sandwiches on the street would never do this no matter even if they weren't fat.

I am the only one who would do this.

Me and Ivan.

Ivan and me.

Lt. Silva and Sunshine grab me firmly by the wrists and begin lowering me into the hole. The others stand guard, over them and over me, but still keep looking back to steal glances. They have me gripped pretty well as they lean in, lean over, lean down, and my vision sees the regular blue and green world rise, then shrink, then become an eighteen-by-eighteen window straight to sky.

The men holding me are extended all the way down. I, too, am extended all the way, hanging on to them, reaching for bottom with my toes.

I have no idea right now, in this mystery shaft, where bottom might be.

"Let me go," I say to the men.

"You feel floor?" Silva says.

"Just drop me," I say. "I'm sure it's here somewhere."

After a two-second pause, which probably involves shrugging, they drop me.

Yeoww. I feel the rush of my organs surprising themselves by surging up through my body, then grunt as I crash to the earth. I figure there was about a six-foot drop between where my feet dangled and where they land. The bump and the surprise of it mean my legs collapse under me when I hit. But I can't even execute a proper fall, since the shaft is too narrow. It's like crash-landing inside a barrel, and I wind up in a semi-crouch.

"Okay?" Silva whispers, and we both know even this much communication could get a guy killed.

"Yeah," I say, and that's the end of that. I can't see anything, so I feel all around me, the moist ancient-scented dirt crumbling in my hands until, in the space behind my knees, I feel where this vertical road turns onto the horizontal one. I twist and torque until I get myself into position, and I'm in.

I lie still for several seconds, listening. Listening for anything at all. I have the semiautomatic pistol in my right hand, and the knife in my left. I don't turn on the flashlight — my neck beam — until I am convinced nobody's going to be staring right at me when I do.

But I feel this much: There is life in here. I can feel this place breathing.

I reach in, like I am about to pinch my own Adam's apple, and snap on the light.

There are *eyes staring right back at me.*

I gasp, and try like a maniac to crawl in reverse. Rats. Rats, rats, which are unpleasant and disgusting when you see them entering the subway at Park Street Station at night, but are *horrors* when they are four inches from your face with fifteen feet of Southeast Asia hanging over you.

I can see one, two, three of them up close, and detect movement farther down, but when I back away like a panicked cockroach it is clear that I am more bothered by the situation than they are. They sniff and stare in my direction, but it doesn't seem like anybody is look-ing to make any false moves. That's what they would say in the gangster movies, *nobody make any false moves*, and since I always found that funny on Sunday afternoon TV, I am going to hang on to that thought while I make my way through this.

Once I am reasonably sure that the situation is as calm as it could be, I reverse direction — and all human impulse — working my way deeper into the tunnel. Right into the teeth of the rats, you might say.

My flesh tingles as I go. *No false moves, guys.* They spread along the edges, up the walls, over my back. That was a false move. That was a very false move. But I push on.

I crawl on my belly for what is probably two hun-dred yards. The rats get routine, even when I can't see them. It is their place. At least it means, if the rats are here, then the snakes probably aren't. There is a famous joke here, that there are about a hundred different vari-eties of snake in Vietnam and ninety-nine of them are poisonous. The other one swallows you whole.

But rats make a good snake early-warning system.

Which is why I get real worried when I realize the rats are gone. All of a sudden, like their mother called them all home for supper, they aren't anywhere to be seen or, more importantly, to be felt.

There is no air down here. I am burning up, but practically liquefying at the same time with the humidity. The only reason I can breathe at all, I imagine, is that there are vents located throughout the system, because these guys thought of pretty much everything. I have even heard that they have small chimneys cut up through the terrain for when they do their cooking. Of course, all of these ingenious airways are also making it possible for all these mosquitoes and spiders and ants and I don't want to think about what elses to be sharing the space with me at this moment.

My skin all over is getting caked with earth. It's starting to feel like I have a coating of soft clay plastered over me, making my pores feel all plugged, making it even harder to feel like I can get a good breath.

I stumble, tumbling into a shallow pool of stagnant water. I don't know what this is for, but it is part of the design because a few yards up I find another, then another. Something to do with preserving the air-chemical mix, I'm guessing, so that life is possible down here. Or possibly basic toilets.

I retch, just a little, thinking I might have just been elbow-deep in VC sewage.

But I push on, and find my first side room. I turn my torso to shine my light in and all around, and see nothing but walls, so I take the turn and explore.

It's about a six-foot side trip into a room the size of a pantry, with rough shelving going up and down the walls. The shelves are piled with cans, empty cans, which, I find when I get up close, are hundreds and hundreds of US C-rations: chili and peaches, corn and creamed beef, and the lot. Either this hotel had American clientele, or we were supplying the enemy without even knowing it.

I keep going. But with every foot of trail I blaze here, I become more convinced this network is as abandoned as the village above it. I do find interesting bits here and there. There is a level down below that was used for trash, and another side room that was used as a bike repair shop. There must be the spare parts to a hundred bikes in here — sprockets, pedals, handlebars, tires, and tubes and bells. The frames of three of them still lean there against the wall, but from the look of it the operation tanked from a critical lack of lubrication. I pick up one chain and it is fused up like a petrified bird skeleton.

In some places I can crouch and shuffle forward instead of crawling on hands and knees, but that's no help and in fact just makes it more frustrating. It makes you want to stand up all the more. Twice, I let the urge get to me and find myself crashing into the rounded dirt ceiling above me. And every time I come to another new dead end of an opening, the entryway is just that much smaller and so I am right back on my knees again.

I smell something different just as I am about to call it quits. Something munitions related. Phosphorus, gunpowder, something.

The opening to this space is slightly larger, and up a bit of a rise. I crawl up a ramp, like to a mini underground parking garage. I flash my light in through the opening and catch a glimpse of a substantial-size storeroom, chock full of the same crates of United States standard ammunition I've been seeing and using since I got here. Our stuff. They got their hands somehow on *our* bullets. They are pumping US personnel full of *our* ammo. Everything from M-60 machine guns to Howitzers to full-metal jacket rounds for this very handgun I am at this very minute —

I get a thump at the base of my neck that feels like a tree falling on me.

I cry out in pain and surprise. I have been clubbed by something like a baseball bat, though it could well be a choice chunk of rock, and my face is being ground into the turf hard enough to make my nose cartilage sound like a bowl of just-wet Rice Krispies amplified inside my head.

There is only one guy, it seems, but one is enough in here. He is on my back and already my light is gone, driven into the dirt. He is grabbing for the knife, smashing my hand against the rocky base of the doorway until the weapon falls out of my grip.

I scramble onto my side, feeling around for the blade while he claws and punches at me, and suddenly, I can tell he's got the bayonet, and we are just smashing and thrashing at each other in pitch blackness, until he grabs me by the neck and we go tumbling down that ramp and away from the underground ammo depot.

We roll backward and crash into what feels like a fork in the tunnel road. I try to wheel on him with the pistol, but it is frankly all guesswork and I'm just flailing around and catching nothing. I stop for a second, listening for his breathing, which is made all but pointless by my own frantic hyperventilating, and I am feeling really in trouble.

Because he knows the terrain.

Whack!

The whole side of my skull feels cracked as he pits the base and blade of my weapon right across my eye socket.

I crash backward again, rolling down to another level, where I bump to a halt against a tunnel wall.

We are both filling the space with breath, and sweat, and fear. He is up above me, I can hear, but I would have to go blindly to go after him at all.

What would the other option be? Waiting?

I crawl up toward his breathing.

He knows every curve down here, for sure. He is up and I am down.

"I'm gonna kill you," I say, dropping my voice as low as I can get it. It's not very low, but I'm just thankful it doesn't crack. "I'm gonna blow your head off, man." Why should I expect him to understand English? Is there any chance in a million scenarios I would be likely to get one word of Vietnamese? I hope my tough John Wayne voice will be enough to defeat him based on tone alone. "Drop that blade, Chucky, or I'm going to shoot you right in the face. I mean it."

"Don't shoot face," he says, from about five feet away and a tick to the left.

"Good," I say, walking forward on my knees. "Good. English. Good. I want to hear the blade hit the ground. I want you to flash that light on the blade where I can see it."

"No light," he says. "You light. No me light."

"You have my light, pal. Don't mess around."

I've stopped. I'm standing, on my knees, with the pistol leveled straight from my shoulder like some kind of dwarf cop busting an invisible drug dealer on the street.

There are three directions he could take, if he wanted to dodge. I haven't the slightest clue.

"I will shoot you," I say.

"Shoot!" he says, and I think I know the spot, so I oblige.

Boom! The sound is deafening in this small space, and as the muzzle flash goes I see the space where I was sure the guy had been. But there is nothing there but ghost.

"I will find you."

He is here, yes, just like a ghost, but I feel his presence like I could feel the rats. I sense him just before he makes his move. He comes through some other side entrance, lunging at me, slicing through my shirt, nicking my shoulder and making me scream at the very same moment I turn on him and pull the trigger.

The gun muzzle bumps right into his head as I shoot him. The flash illuminates his face at the very instant the blast tears it right off his skull.

I sit. In the darkest darkness there is.

That face. It was with me, for a fragment of a fragment of a second that face was here in the world with my face and now they are in very different places.

How old was he? Who can tell with these guys? As far as I can tell they are ageless, and probably won't ever die if you don't blow them away at some point.

Might have been a kid. Might have been younger than me. Why was he here by himself? Was he abandoned, or punished, or rewarded for his bravery and independence? Was he here by accident? I used to think I was here by accident. Now I know I was all the way wrong about that.

Who was he?

Why should I care?

Point-blank. I can only imagine what this scene looks like right here. A bloody mess.

Or no mess at all. Beck used to drive me demented with that thing about if a tree falls in the forest does anybody hear it. Teased me like when you feed a crazy dog his own tail so he'll chase it 'til he drills himself into the ground.

Maybe that tree doesn't make a noise, though. And maybe if you blow a kid's face off in the dark under the ground then it makes no mess.

I have to get back.

It's also probably a good thing I won't be reading any kind of map to get myself back, because then I'd never get there. As it is, I think I know the way. Like I know the rats are here and like the rats know where they're going, I think I'll be fine without any eyes.

"I have to go, man," I say to him. After you kill somebody, I am finding, you have a sort of warm feeling about them. I suppose it would be different if it was somebody you killed because you hated them. But I haven't had that. I've only killed the people I'm supposed to kill.

"You keep the bayonet," I say, even though it strictly didn't belong to me. It strictly does belong to him now.

I don't know how long the whole trip has been, time-wise, by the time I grab the rope and the guys pull me up into the light. Like a lot of these missions and these moments here in Vietnam, I think it probably felt like a lot longer than it actually took in real time.

"Oh, *man*," Hunter says, coming right up to me as soon as I'm out of the ground. "Are you all right?"

"All the way all right," I say brightly.

Lt. Silva is staring at me, his look both intense and distant.

"Here's your gun, boss," I say. As I hand it over, I see it's absolutely laminated in shiny red blood. As is my hand.

"Sorry, Sunshine," I say, "but I don't have your bayonet. I seem to have lost a couple of things down there."

"Uh-huh," he says, looking at me just a tiny bit less dominating than before. "Kill anybody while you were at it?"

I look down at my hands, all glistening in that hot, wicked sun. Then I look back up at him.

"It was so dark down there, man, who could tell?"

That's what I say. I'm just a bit surprised to hear myself say it. But it beats what I want to say.

What I want to tell them all is: Yeah, I killed somebody. I killed Rudi.

Old Rudi, or maybe Young Rudi.

No. Rudy-Judy is who he was. But he's not anymore. Killed him and left him right down in that hole.

That's what I want to say. But I know how weird that would sound, so I keep it to myself.

CHAPTER TEN

Disconnected

I have a *what*?"

The corporal, who I have never seen before, laughs at my shock.

"You heard me right, private," he says. "You have a call. Follow me, please."

I follow him — at a trot, because apparently these things are time sensitive. He leads me to a tent that's got all kinds of wires running in and out of it, then inside to a squeezed-up desk in the corner among a lot of other squeezed-up desks and guys with headphones on. I grab a phone receiver.

"Yeah?" I say.

"Well, it is about time."

"Morris?" I say. I don't know what I was expecting, but it wasn't this. "Morris, man, is that you?"

"It's me, Rudi, man. So good to hear your voice."

"Same here, Morris."

"I was starting to think I'd never get a hold of you. How are you doing?"

"Great, Morris, I'm doing great. What about you?"

"Well, I wouldn't say great, but all right. I'm surviving, getting by, you know. That's the best we can do over here, isn't it?"

I'm surprised at how much like a corporal he sounds. "What? No. Actually, no. You can do a lot better than that."

"Oh. You can? Oh, so I guess when you said you were fitting in with the Marines, you meant you really were —"

"What else could I have meant?"

"All right, all right," he says. "You're awful edgy all of a sudden."

"And you're awfully sensitive all of a sudden. All I was saying, Morris, was that if more of our guys over here wanted to get something accomplished, instead of just wanting to get by and then get out, maybe we'd have won this thing already. We talk about it here all the time, that Charlie's like the thing that wouldn't die. No matter how many days we blast him away we come back the next day and there he is. I don't see him quitting like I see a lot of our guys doing. The VC, man, those guys ain't messing around, and they ain't just waiting to go home, either."

"That's 'cause they *are* home."

"Hnnn. Maybe. Anyway, have you seen this book thing the Defense Department produces? It's called *Know Your Enemy: The Vietcong.*"

"Ah, gee, Rude, not yet. . . . I think it's in the stack on my nightstand."

"Hey, be a wiseguy if you want, but if you read it you would know just how prepared and committed these guys are. They got these lists, their oath, their twelve rules of discipline, their rules of attention — rules of *attention*, man! If they weren't the enemy, I might have to start hanging around with them instead of some of the people we got here."

There is a silence on the other end of the line, which, combined with his silence while I was talking, is a lot of nothing coming from the guy who actually made the call.

"What's the matter with you?" I say, and I hear more impatience in my voice than I intend, but, oh well.

"I was just going to ask you the same question. You don't sound like yourself, Rudi, to be honest."

"Good," I say loudly. "Thank you. Because you know what? I'm not that guy. The Marines have remade me, Morris. I've remade myself. The Rudi you knew was a loser, man, and good riddance to him."

"No, no, no," he says, matching my intensity for the first time in the conversation. "The Rudi I knew was an excellent guy. He was kind of a goof, but he was somebody loveable. And I know I speak for the other guys, too, when I say I would rather you came home a good guy and a bad soldier than the other way around."

The radio coordinator guy comes over to me and starts tapping his watch already. I turn away from him.

"Morris, are you not paying attention? Are you even bothering to read my letters? I'm not going home. Understand? I mean, you guys are still the best guys in the world, and we will always be us no matter what, but . . . I'm not going back home. I *hate* home. The Marines is my home, where I fit and where I belong. If they keep fighting in Vietnam then that's where I'll be. If they fight on into China, look for me there. If the Russians want a piece, bring it on 'cause I'll be there. Boston can just take a hike. If I never see that place again that's just fine with me. In fact, I would really like it if the USMC declared war on Massachusetts. That would thrill me all over."

He's gone all silent again. But because he is Morris I know the silence doesn't stand a chance.

"How 'bout your mom, Rudi? Don't you want to go home to your mom?"

I should show more respect here but, you know, this just isn't the time.

"Mom? *My* mom? Okay, right, I missed her when I left. And I was thinking about her at first, before I started getting experienced, y'know, started turning into a man and into a Marine. Then, I got reality, Morris."

"You got reality."

"Reality, right. And reality is this. I needed my mom because I was nobody, with nothing, understand? Then I got to be somebody and I found myself needing less and less of Mom, or anybody, really. And I realized, a big part of why I was Mr. Nobody with Nothing, was 'cause of her."

"Ah, Rudi, man, she did her best —"

"Know how many letters I've gotten from my mother? None. But I'm not surprised. She told me that was how it would be. The day I left, man, my mother — my own mother — said that because I was me it was so sure that I was gonna get killed that she was considering me dead as soon as she shut the door. That way she could protect herself from all the worrying, and if I came back someday it would just be a pleasant surprise. Huh? How's that for a pat on the back, a confidence booster on the way to war? Well, what she doesn't know is that that Rudi, Rudy-Judy, is dead already, and this Rudi that has replaced him is invincible. So there."

There is another silence out there, this one longer. And again, because I know Morris like I do, I can just about see him.

"You're shaking your head now, right? And holding your hand flat up against your forehead."

This, at least, brings a chuckle out of him.

"I see you've invented the picture phone," he says.

And now I chuckle, and now that has to be good enough to end on.

"Anyway, you may be a privileged radioman with all the time in the world, Morris, but I have a guy here waiting to unplug me."

"Remember who and what you are, Rudi. Remember most of all what you are *not*. And then go and be everything else."

"Morris, if you start talking to me like Beck then I will pull the plug here myself."

He sighs loudly. "I know you've killed people, Rude. Maybe a lot —"

"A lot." No sense in tiptoeing.

"But you don't have to become one of them. That doesn't have to be who you are. You're not —"

"I am."

"You also never used to —"

"Interrupt you?" I laugh, and he does, too.

It feels really, really, really good to be laughing, blending laughs with one of the guys. I'm shocked at the feeling it gives me. Frightened by it, even.

It's a feeling connected to old stuff, and that feeling has to go.

"I have to go," I say.

"No, don't."

"I have to, Morris, because they're gonna disconnect me."

And I also have to because I have to. Before Morris disconnects me. Disconnects *me*. I start talking very fast, so that I can get my words in, and so that he can't.

"There is order here, Morris, and I understand it. I am good at this, and I am making a difference. I control stuff like I never could, and like I never will, outside of this thing. There will be no twelve-months-and-out for me. I'm in, all the way in, forever. I hope you understand, and I hope Beck understands, but I *know* that Ivan understands. And he's proud of me, and by the time I'm done he's gonna be even prouder, wait and see."

"I can promise you that Ivan is in no way —"

I pull the receiver away from my ear when I see the radioman walking briskly toward me and waving his hands in front of his face like he's disallowing a touchdown.

"Rudi!" I hear little-voice Morris bellowing at me desperately.

"Yeah, Morris," I say, buying one more moment from the radioman with one finger in the air.

"You don't have to like what you have to do here. You're not *supposed* to like it."

"Well, there ya go," I say. "When did I ever do anything the way I was supposed to?"

"Wait, we're all very —"

Morris is still talking at me when I hand the phone over voluntarily and get back to business.

CHAPTER ELEVEN

Disordered

Co Co Village?" I say when Silva tells us the assignment. It's a special one — I can tell because he has come over to our hooch to fill it up with his smoke. That's a first. "But lieutenant, there's nothing to do there. The CAP guys have it all packed up tight and passive. What, did they run out of candy and flower seeds?"

"As a matter of fact I think they have run out of candy and flower seeds. But as it happens they are also running low on men."

"Why's that, lieutenant?" Sunshine asks.

"That is because, I'm afraid things aren't going so well. Not in Co Co, and not with the CAP program in I Corps generally. They are getting hit more often, and more strategically. Locals are getting more distant, and the guys who aren't local — that would be Charlie — are getting less distant."

"We're losing, is that what you're saying?" Sunshine, like Silva, is not one for beating around bushes. They speak the same language.

"I am not saying that, private. But I am coming close to saying it. In a couple of weeks, in fact, we're pulling the CAP program out of Co Co village."

"For good?" Hunter asks.

"For good."

Sunshine, Hunter, and myself are gathered around the lieutenant now like we're kids at story time, in a cloud of cigarette smoke. Marquette remains on his bunk.

"You getting all this, Marquette?" Lt. Silva asks.

"Every word, lieutenant," he answers as sleeplike as he can.

"Good. Then you, and all of us, can start packing up, because we are moving on down the road. They have lost three men, and we are providing them with seven to make up for it in these final weeks of the program. The five of us, along with Corporals Cherry and McClean, are going to be CAPs for a while. Whole new world, huh?"

Lt. Silva has finally managed to get all of Marquette's attention. He sits up, swings his feet to the floor.

"Lieutenant, how exactly does a CAP unit *lose* three men?"

Silva sticks his cigarette into his teeth, that skeleton-effect thing he does so well. He holds up a thumb. "One was shot with an AK-47 by an eleven-year-old." He keeps his thumb extended and adds the index finger. "One was blown up by a booby-trapped radio." He adds another finger. "And one did the bamboo snake two-step." It is called *the bamboo two-step* because the snake is so poisonous that you only get two steps before you fall down dead. "Although, that terminology may not be fitting in this case since the soldier was sitting down at the time of the biting and so he didn't take any steps at all. And since the viper in question came out of a bag of freshly, locally laundered uniforms, one might be inclined to move that one also into the booby-trap column. Needless to say, the CAP unit is no longer patronizing the local laundress. Nor any of the other small local businesses that had been heretofore benefiting from Uncle Sam's haphazard generosity. This state of affairs is consequently doing very little to sustain good relations on either side."

"And *that's* where we're going?" Hunter asks. Fairly enough.

"Yes, it is."

"Why?" Sunshine asks.

Lt. Silva shrugs. "I think the president referred to it as 'an honorable end to the war.'"

"What does that mean?" Hunter asks.

"It means we ain't leaving 'til we say we're leaving," I say.

Silva nods at me. "Yeah, something like that. The Marines have set their withdrawal date from the village, and we don't look good if we get pushed out early. With a little effort and luck we might be able to leave the place a little more pacified and friendly than it is at this moment."

You can feel the energy wafting out of the place along with Silva's cloud as he leaves the hooch. This is a tough one, high on difficulty and low on potential for success. What would success even look like? But we are Marines. So, first thing in the morning, we will march.

"Good luck with that," Marquette says, lying back on his bunk.

The three of us turn as one on him.

"What are you saying?" Hunter asks, befuddled.

"I'm saying shut up, Hunter, that's what I'm saying."

Sunshine takes one slow, sure step in the direction of Marquette's bunk. Marquette smiles broad and slimy. "Go, on, big boy," he says, "go right ahead. Do me the biggest favor of the whole war. Only this time put a little more effort into it so I can go home. Save me the trouble of doing it myself. 'Cause one way or another, you boys are definitely going to Co Co village without me."

And in that moment, if I was going to build a thing in my mad-scientist laboratory that would bring out all the hatred and hostility in my soul, that thing would come out looking and sounding and acting just like Marquette.

We're all lying in our bunks, and it's a quiet night in Chu Lai. When it's like this, the warm dark night sitting on top of us like blankets, frogs and insects making the loudest noises on the slightly stirring air, this place could be like a home almost. Or, anyway, like a summer-vacation camp where a guy could close his eyes and just be all right, trusting that his fellow campers all around him are having the same good time, sharing the same dreams tonight for the same outcomes tomorrow.

But I tip a glance over in the direction of Marquette's bunk and I know it just won't ever be that here. He is going to be a rat, and he's going to get away with it, though I don't know how. We hear stories about guys doing all kinds of crazy stuff to injure themselves out of fighting duty, and Marquette could easily be one of those guys. He's already snoring, so he's obviously not sweating it like I am.

I look over to Hunter, who is staring at the ceiling and worrying himself to sleep. I stare over at Sunshine, who looks to be sleeping and readying himself for what's to come tomorrow. Which should be plenty.

"Hey! Hey, hey!" Before I even know I am asleep, I wake up to almighty screaming coming from Marquette's bunk.

"Shut up, will ya?" Sunshine bellows back. It is just breaking dawn, and all of us are awake, just like that. "I wasn't done sleeping yet, Marquette, you jerk. Neither were these guys. Now, look, you got everybody up, and we all have a big day today."

It is quite a scene. Sunshine's bed has at sometime during the night made its way across the floor to butt up against Marquette's. Marquette is swinging and flailing around, but not getting much accomplished, because Sunshine is shadowing his every move.

He has no choice but to shadow him, really, since they are shackled together, right ankle to left, right wrist to left.

Hunter starts falling all over the place laughing, and I join him. Sunshine deserves credit for keeping a completely straight face but Marquette deserves none because being deadly serious right now is no effort for him at all.

"What do you think you're doing?" Marquette barks.

"Being a good Marine, and a good buddy," Sunshine says.

"Get these things off of me, Gillespie, I mean it."

"Sure thing," Sunshine says. "But we gotta go find my friend, who's an MP on patrol duty. You know, Military Police? He's got the key. And lucky for you he understands your sleepwalking problem. I explained the whole thing to him."

"I don't sleepwalk," Marquette says. The two of them are now standing in the middle of the hooch in their skivvies.

"Not with your buddy Sunshine looking out for you," Sunshine says, smiling.

"Listen to me, Sunshine. . . ."

All the humor falls away like a five-hundred-pound bomb off a B-52.

"Don't call me that. You hear me?"

I think at this point if Marquette called him Sir, Your Majesty, or Handsome, Gillespie would still threaten his life.

And no matter how badly Marquette would like to get himself injured and exempt himself from our mission, it is very clear he doesn't want it bad enough to let Gillespie do the honors now.

"Yeah. I hear ya."

"Now, it's a lovely morning. Too late to go back to sleep now, what with the hike we gotta take and all. Let's you and me go find that key, huh?"

"Yeah," Marquette says glumly. "I guess."

Sunshine has a spring in his step as he exits the hooch. Marquette is stepping with a lot more care and caution.

"Don't you worry," Sunshine says to him, "I did a little freelance night patrol out here, cleaned up any little hazards that were lurking around between here and, oh, say the latrine. Shocking, how dangerous a place this can be, don't ya think, Marquette?"

"Yeah," he says, sounding more depressed every second.

"Good thing we're moving out of this neighborhood, huh? I can guarantee I'll keep you absolutely safe from harm between now and then."

Hunter and I laugh and slap palms at the great morning floor show, then, as if we've heard a bell go off at the same time, we both settle right back down.

Sunshine said it. We're moving out.

"Is that what I think it is?" I ask Cpl. McClean, even though it's the kind of question that's really the opposite of a question.

He has a flamethrower strapped to his back. And so does Cpl. Cherry.

"Yup," he says.

"Why?"

"Because it's been requested, that's why."

Holy moly.

As it turns out, we're all loaded for bear. Everyone packs his own M-16, of course, but is also equipped with a variety of grenades and Claymore mines. In addition, each of us is weighed down with an extra weapon, either a shoulder-mounted rocket launcher or an M-60 machine gun, and all the extra ammo that goes with it. Because we're headed to a village and not a bivouac situation out in the field, we don't have to waste rucksack space on silly things like food or any more than one canteen of water each.

Good thing, too. As it is, this is the heaviest pack I have ever marched with.

"Are we taking over a country by ourselves?" McClean asks Silva as we start down the road.

"Just being cautious," the lieutenant answers crisply. And with finality.

It is, as they mostly are and should be, a pretty quiet hike. The sun's beating madly, right down through the canopy as we walk single-file along the trail we know better than any other in our whole area of operations. I'm not quite sure how much talking we would do today even if we could. I, for one, don't feel like chatting.

Silva-McClean-Hunter-Cherry-Marquette-Sunshine-Me. That's our formation for the march, and I have to believe Marquette is the most uncomfortable man in Vietnam at this moment. He did not want to be here, does not want to march, is just as nervous as anybody about the assignment.

And scariest of all, he's listening to Sunshine's thumping bootsteps right behind him.

I like my position. I once thought of rear guard as last place, but that's not right. Rear guard is important. Rear guard suits me. March along, looking straight and left and right like everybody else, then every so often do a complete scan of the terrain behind us. I don't get nervous about being the last line of defense with no backup. In fact, it revs me up, sharpens my senses, makes me smarter.

Thump-thump-thump-thump, the rhythm of the day gives me strength. No words. I love no words. Eyes on the prize and shut up, that's what I like. I'm in such a groove after the first twenty minutes, I'm practically meditating.

And not thinking about something I should have been thinking about.

The spot. It comes up on us with no warning. Because why should there be any warning? It's a sweaty green dense patch of jungle just like a zillion other sweaty green dense patches of jungle, and while I don't sense it as we approach, I surely sense it every which way when we pass close by it.

My deathplace birthplace.

It's where it happened. We all march on, nobody noticing but me. Because it's mine, and means nothing at all to anybody else despite the guys here who witnessed it and the guys here who set it up.

That, right there, in that small thicket, against that tree.

March, march, march, sweat, march . . .

I killed a man for the first time, right there, and I swear it could have happened six seconds ago. I am heart-racing like a jackrabbit as I turn my head to look, like he's right there, looking back at me, trying to hold his guts in, trying to pull away from the tree, from the wires cutting into his ankles and his wrists while I was cutting into his abdomen, and then his throat.

It could be happening *right this second*, with the way I am outsweating everybody by ten, outbreathing, outpulsating, outmarching —

"Hey, nutso," Sunshine says to me in a whisper-growl.

I have walked right into him, stepped on the heel of his boot and found myself with my nose all but stuck in the muzzle of the M-60 he has slung over his back.

"Sorry," I say, "sorry, sorry."

We're a half mile farther down the road before I stop checking over my shoulder every three seconds. He would have every right. To come after me. Every right.

But if he did, I'd kill him all over again. That's just how it is.

Uneventful. Despite what was going on in my head part of the way, that's how our march to Co Co village turns out.

"And let's hope that's how the whole two weeks go," Lt. Silva says as he shakes hands with our host, Sgt. Culverhouse.

"Two weeks?" Culverhouse says, surprised. "Lieutenant, I like your optimism, but at this point every time we go two *hours* without our head count dropping that's a cause for celebration."

We are standing in the spot outside the sergeant's quarters where we have stood before, dropping off candy and comic books and other goodies to the locals and winning the hearts and minds of this village. But it feels like a different place. No kids have come running out to greet us, no old men or women pass by going about the business of just being folks. The village itself, the terrain, is not what it was but instead a dried and stripped-down poor faded version of a place that's been gradually trampled into dust. It's dusty, is the big difference. And motionless.

"Where are your numbers going?" Silva asks.

Culverhouse motions for us to follow into his quarters. Inside there is a bed that's pretty large by military standards, a small kitchen with a bamboo table and four chairs. There is a desk with a chair in a living area with two bamboo three-seater couches. We spread ourselves around as Culverhouse takes the seat behind the desk, like a judge ruling over his court.

Lt. Silva lights up and offers the sergeant a cigarette, which he declines.

"Pretty plush, as these places go," Silva says.

"You outrank me, so it's all yours. I can be packed and out of here in fifteen minutes."

"Thanks anyway," Silva says. "But I'm just a guest. So, about your numbers?"

"Aside from the casualties? We've had desertions. And people stopped volunteering for this program some time ago because it got a reputation as a kind of suicide mission. So we've had an attrition problem. We lost people who never got replaced. Until eventually the numbers got a little uncomfortably low and, like jackals, Charlie started to sniff us out. Farm country," he gestures in a circular motion all around. "We're surrounded by farms. Which was great when we had the locals on our side."

"But if you don't have them . . ."

"Staging areas. Hiding places and launch pads. We are under siege here, lieutenant, on three sides. That road you just came up is the exception."

There are low groans coming from members of our party. Until Lt. Silva stands up and lays a very impressive mass scowl on the room.

"So, I have to ask," Silva says, "what are we supposed to do?"

Sgt. Culverhouse suddenly pulls down a face like he's pulling down a dark window shade. He looks immediately sadder and more tired than before he had heard that inevitable question. He gets up out of his desk chair and comes around to the lieutenant with his fingers scissoring for that cigarette.

"We are going to *achieve peace with honor.*"

Guys here really seem to hate that phrase.

"Leave with our tails between our legs," Cpl. Cherry blurts.

"No, no," the sergeant says, dropping down with a thump back into his chair. "That's what you guys are for. You guys and your firepower make it possible for us to proudly leave with our tails *up* in the air."

"Sheesh," Lt. Silva says.

"Ya," Culverhouse says. "I know, sheesh. The CAP program was a good program. The best. It was working. We were winning the hearts and minds of the people, until we just started running out of steam. It's a shame, a real shame. So, what we are left with is this. A couple of our remaining Vietnamese partners, the Popular Force soldiers, will be here in the morning. The PF guys, by the way, are useless at this point, which is a huge part of our problem. There is absolutely no way of telling whose side they are on. Anyway, they will be here in the morning, along with the regional chieftain of the surrounding area, to discuss our departure. Our hope is that we can convince them that although we won't be here on-site anymore, that we are right down the road. You guys will stand around like mafia types to illustrate this. Hopefully, they get the message that we could come back any time we wanted — or any time *they* wanted — so they don't absolutely have to go over to the VC. We're not completely giving up on them."

"Wow," Silva says, hearing the same exhaustion we can all hear in the sergeant's voice. "I'm on your side, and even I don't believe you."

The sergeant nods and shrugs at the same time. "All there is to do between now and then is to maintain our presence, walk regular patrols — *within* the village boundaries, we don't go out anymore — and enjoy the scenery, boys."

Before there's any more talk of enjoying the scenery, we get set up in our quarters. The seven of us are divided into three huts roughly the same size as the sergeant's setup, right near his at the edge of the village. The rest of the CAP Marines are divided over a few more structures clustered nearby so that the total American presence huddles together just at the spot where you'd enter the village — or just where you'd bolt from it. It's like the last few houses on a street that's gradually being abandoned by the neighborhood.

Lt. Silva has a place to himself while the corporals and Marquette take one place and me, Hunter, and Sunshine take another.

Unpacking basically amounts to selecting a bunk, taking our big artillery and laying it under the bed, then lying down, each of us with an M-16 either nestled beside him or placed right across his chest. My roommates and I have our afternoon rest just this way.

"This little vacation can't be over quick enough for my liking," Hunter says.

Sunshine sighs deeply. "There is an air of futility settled over this whole thing, isn't there?"

"Doesn't feel good," I say, "that's for sure."

"Right, gentlemen," a voice snaps through the room. We all jump up, rifles ready, and see the grunt at the door. It's Cpl. Krug, the CAP soldier I met way back when he was giving some old VC guy a going-over. "Who's first up for patrol?"

We are pairing with the established guys, doing the rounds every couple of hours. Gives us a chance to get to know the place, while it gives them the opportunity to start kissing it good-bye.

Since Krug and I are old pals, I figure this is my turn.

"I thought I trusted these people, I really did," he says as the two of us saunter down what you would call the main strip of the village. We walk very slowly, and turn left and right regularly like a pair of cuckoo-clock birds, looking into every window and alleyway.

"I guess that's over with now?" I say.

"Ha." He spits out a laugh. "The worst of all are those PF rats. They played us great. Fellow soldiers, yeah right. They were playing all sides for what they could get. Those are the guys, if they just let us have a shot . . ."

I find myself very aware, now, of all the people I do not see outside. Two women pass by, carrying empty buckets in the direction of the small stream running alongside the edge of the village. Off in the distance two older men, hunched, are heading for the farm on the hill up the road. I see nobody else. Small heads appear in windows then disappear so quickly I can't even tell if they are adults or not. To be honest I might not be able to tell even if I got a longer look. I believe at this point I will wind up leaving this country without the ability to reliably tell the ages of the locals within a margin of error of twenty years. And I don't even know what I think about that.

"Yeah yeah, keep staring!" Cpl. Krug shouts as one more head slips from view in a window in a half-collapsed hut on the far lip of the village. We stand there for a minute, looking out past our imaginary boundary, into the rolling countryside beyond. "There," he says, pointing to one fenced-in field with two buffalo standing like sculptures. "And there. And that one and the one up top there."

"What are those?"

"Those are VC hyena packs. Established, committed, just waiting for us to get weak enough or to fade away entirely so they can swoop in. These people ain't never coming over to our side, never listening to what we have to say. We shouldn't even be talking to them at this point. We should just mortar and rocket and strafe the life out of 'em on the way out the door. After all we did for this community, it's an insult to the effort to leave the whole show to the VC after we've gone. And I can tell you, every last man here feels the same."

Sounds pretty extreme to me.

But it doesn't sound wrong.

Cpl. Krug executes a neat heel turn, and we're headed back to our end of town again.

"How was that, then?" Sunshine asks over the card game he's playing with Hunter.

"*Swell* would be the only word to do it justice," I say. They have a small transistor radio going, and somebody delivered bowls of rice and some kind of cubed meat while I was out. If you didn't know what we, maybe, know, you might think this wasn't such a bad little holiday right here. "I might consider buying a vacation home in this community after this is done," I say.

"Not me," says Hunter, taking it all as seriously as possible. Fair enough.

"Who's next?" says another corporal standing in the doorway, just as grim and unsmiling as the last.

And the next.

And the next.

By the time it is my turn to patrol again, it's dusky, and Krug is standing in the doorway, drumming his fingers impatiently on the frame.

We walk the same walk, see even fewer people, have

possibly the same conversation all over again. There are no lights coming on in the huts, no candles or flashlights or anything. The frogs and night birds and other wildlife are getting into voice, though, so it's almost as if the place has twice the life it did in the daytime. Which wouldn't be hard.

Crrr-racck! A single rifle shot fractures the evening air. I feel the bullet whistle right past me.

"Yaaaaahhh!" Krug screams, cupping a hand to the side of his head just below his helmet. Absolute gushings of blood are pouring out through his fingertips and down the side of his face. I grab him by the shoulder and haul him down the middle of the village, like we are in some arcade game where every last person in the village is allowed to have a shot at us.

We are motoring wildly until we see the medic, a Navy Corpsman, running out of one of the huts with a roll of gauze already in his hand. There are three other grunts around him, covering me and Krug as we run the village gauntlet. Nobody is shooting at us now, though, and I can't even tell if anybody is bothered enough to come to the windows or doors to gawk. When we reach the men, the Corpsman slaps the whole roll of gauze onto the side of Krug's head and they wrestle him inside.

"He shot my ear off!" Krug says as he staggers into the hut.

I go to follow, and one of the CAP guys stops me with a hand like a traffic cop. "We got it, private," he says flat as the ocean. "You should get yourself back inside."

And just like that I find myself outside, alone, in this strange, strange, strange place. I take a couple of walking steps in the direction of my quarters, and then I run full out.

Hunter and Sunshine are waiting and basically drag me into the hut.

"What's happening, man?" Sunshine says.

"Sniper," I say, breathless. "Jeez, you know, it's just a guy with a gun, but is there anything really scarier than a sniper, man?"

"No," they say together, "no, no."

"Anyway," I say, "one of them shot that guy Krug's ear off. The medic is working on him now. Say, whose turn is it for patrol?"

"Wait, first, where'd the shot come from?" Sunshine snaps. "Was it inside the village or out?"

I start to give him an answer, but then realize I haven't got one. "I don't even know, man. Could have been inside."

"Ahhh," they both say, backing away with their hands up like captured prisoners.

Lt. Silva appears in the doorway. "You all right?" he asks me.

"Sure. Don't think I'll sleep very well here tonight, though."

"Yeah," he says, nodding and smoking. "I'm going to go talk to the sarge. Whatever happens, don't anybody go outside without direct orders from me. Understood?"

"I understood it before you even said it," Hunter says, and the three of us head back into the corner, where we sit on bunks, try and play cards while we listen to the radio.

The radio is on low, but it could be over loudspeakers the way it is cutting through everything. We would rather listen to it than anything else right now, but we know, as soldiers, we need to hear more than music. Sunshine turns the volume down lower. The music is whispering to us now, but at the same time the rest of the world outside has turned down its volume as well.

It is creepy-eerie, and the tension is flammable.

"We have to be able to retaliate, whether we get the order or not," Sunshine says.

"If it was up to me," I say, "I'd vote we pre-taliate."

"Works for me," says Sunshine. "Too bad this hut is full of good Marines who follow orders."

I look at him hard now, thinking back to past events. "You are, aren't you? In spite of whatever makes you mad. You are a soldier who follows orders, even stupid ones."

"Even stupid ones."

"Even bad leaders, you follow."

"Unfortunately," he sighs. "Even bad ones."

"Well, the guy in the next hut is a fine leader," I say, pointing my thumb in the direction of where Silva and Culverhouse are having their high-level strategy meeting.

"Agreed," he says.

I don't even know what card game we're supposed to be playing. Hunter just keeps going around and around and dealing out the entire deck of cards. So that must mean, War.

Out in the distance, there are noises. Something like animal noises, like owls, wolves, hyenas, and even whale song, coming down on us out of the hills and fields.

"Jeepers," Hunter says, shaking as he turns over a card.

"Hang tough, man," Sunshine says. He's sitting on his bunk, while we're sitting on Hunter's. We're using an upturned five-gallon plastic drum for a card table. Sunshine flips a card over and casually reaches under his bed for his M-60 machine gun.

I flip a card and then slip over to my bunk and get mine, while Hunter reaches down for his. It's as though we have been bunked according to weaponry, and this is the machine gunners' dormitory. If nothing else, there won't be any bunch that's going to outdo the three of us in rounds per second.

This might be the world's most high-strung low-stakes game of cards. The three of us players randomly turning over cards, each weighed down with two major weapons, bandoliers, and a backpack full of more ammo.

"Eagle," Hunter says, bringing a whole new game into play. "I hear eagle."

"I hear monkey screech," Sunshine says.

"I got loon," I add. "That's a talented bunch out there."

It helps a little, making light of the terror. But, also, it doesn't. The calls are distant, but somehow all the spookier for it.

All of our cards are now down on the drum staring up stupidly at us while we stare stupidly down at them. And softly softly softly, The Lovin' Spoonful sing up to us, "Darling Be Home Soon," and because this makes as much sense as anything, Hunter says, "Go Fish."

Bang! Ba-bang! B-B-B-B-B-B-B-BANNNGGGG!

It has kicked off, and it has kicked off full throttle and right here in little Co Co Village. The sound, a nonstop wall of shooting, sounds like the rifle range in basic when the whole camp was going at it at once.

Bu-hooom!

And the RPGs are out. It's all happening on our doorstep, a true-life, door-to-door, hand-to-hand battle for this sad little village.

"What do we do?" I ask Sunshine.

The three of us are up and ready and bouncing up and down on the balls of our feet by the door. But we hold on, waiting.

"Let's go!" the lieutenant and the sergeant holler as they fly past the door toward the action.

So, we go.

We make our way hut by hut upward through the village the same way Krug and I went on our patrol. There is a monstrous amount of gunfire happening at the village's far end where Krug was shot, but I'm surprised to find we don't seem to be taking any incoming from the hot spots around the village.

"What's happening?" I ask as we duck behind the last of the "American" huts. What is certain is that all our guys, CAP and regular grunts, are already going at it heavily with the enemy somewhere up ahead. Every last man is gone out of these huts, even Krug.

Maybe especially Krug.

"Somebody kicked something off," Lt. Silva says.

"I told my men to hold fire," Sgt. Culverhouse says. "Krug was being taken care of. It was probably a rogue shooter. I ordered my men to suspend patrols, to let it cool down and let us get to this meeting in the morning."

"So what happened?" Sunshine says.

"What do you think, soldier?" Culverhouse says.

"Your men waited for you to get around the corner, then they went out hunting."

Culverhouse puts his index finger on the tip of his nose and presses it flat.

Bingo.

The sergeant heads up-village, still ducking in a hut at a time, but it is obvious where the action is.

We can tell by the trail.

Bodies are appearing in the road. They are hanging out through windows. At least a half dozen uniformed Americans are visible between the spot where we stand and where the remaining soldiers are making a stand seventy yards farther up. Two huts up, there is a hut completely bombed out with at least ten bodies smoldering about the place. Small bodies, but man, I will never be able to read these people, so I don't know. A hut down the road is a bonfire.

As we near the first American bodies, Hunter points down at Marquette, spread in the road.

"I'm surprised he even bothered to come this far," I say.

Sunshine points his M-60 at the body, but doesn't shoot. He does better.

"You think this is bad," he says to the dead man, "wait 'til Lieutenant Jupp gets his ghostly hands on ya."

But the joke evaporates just that quickly as we take in all the dead Marines.

We don't need orders now. We all run.

Hunter, Sunshine, and I are pouring M-60 rounds into everybody and anybody on the opposite side of the line from our guys, who are squatting, kneeling, lying down on one side of the road, set up in the windows of three huts they have commandeered. They are stepping over dead Vietnamese, pushing them aside. Somebody hurls a body into the street and it's so light it sails almost into the hut opposite.

Just as we arrive, Cpl. Cherry screams like crazy and opens up his flamethrower and instantly sends two huts shooting red into the sky. Three Vietnamese men with guns come running out completely in flames, and all the firepower of the USMC steps in to do the humane thing and put them so far out of their misery that the pieces divide into thirty or forty small little fires right there in the road in front of us. I see movement, and I shoot it. I see another movement, and I shoot it.

VC? Who can say for sure?

Free-fire zone.

The CAP world was once the very opposite of the free-fire world.

Free-fire.

It is very close to silent in my head now, though everybody everywhere is firing as if any unused ammunition will be turned on us as punishment. The sounds — of explosions and screams, and of that peculiar hot flapping sheet of fire — are all adding up to a kind of silence, as I watch my fingers, my hands, my arms, doing the hard muscular work of killing that person there, and that one and that one until every bit of this job is done and I can stop.

That silence, the one made up of all the sounds, continues and continues and continues long after there ceases to be any movement on the other side of the line. The heat of it all is what finally blows me backward, away from the fight that isn't any fight anymore.

As I walk back to my quarters, to get my good night's sleep before the big meeting in the morning, I finally hear a sound. It's the helicopters, coming to evacuate us all from this place tonight.

Confirmed kills.

Co Co Village. Confirmed.

CHAPTER TWELVE

No More Casualties

I never was good with letters anyway, so this is better.

I've stopped writing letters to my pals. It's hard to make yourself understood by writing letters, when you're a guy like me. Even to your best pals. They can't understand.

So I keep it simple now. Everybody always told me that, anyway. *Just keep it simple, Rudi.*

So I don't write letters now.

I write numbers.

> DEAR IVAN,
> 24.
> 25.
> 26.
> YOUR PAL,
> RUDI

About the Author

Chris Lynch is the author of numerous acclaimed books for middle-grade and teen readers, including the Cyberia series and the National Book Award finalist *Inexcusable*. He teaches in the Lesley University creative writing MFA program, and divides his time between Massachusetts and Scotland.